Once upon a time...

ON MOUNTAINTOP ROCK

by John McLay

COBBLESTONE
CREEK

National Library of Canada Cataloguing in Publication Data

McLay, John, 1947 –

On Mountaintop Rock

ISBN 0-9688467-0-X

1. Jasper Region (Alta.) – History – Fiction.

2. Rocky Mountains, Canadian (B.C. and Alta.) – History – Fiction. I. Title

PS8575.L367O5 2001   C813'.6   C2001-900100-2   PR9199.3.M33154O5 2001

Published in Canada in 2001 by

Cobblestone Creek Publishing

6528-112 Street,   Edmonton, AB

T6H 4R2

Phone 434-8217   Fax 434-8221

jmclay@interbaun.com

Grateful acknowledgment to the estate of Sir Arthur Conan Doyle for permission to use excerpts from his work.

"Bali Ha'i", "Happy Talk", "I'm Gonna Wash That Man Right Outa My Hair", "Some Enchanted Evening" and "A Wonderful Guy" by Richard Rodgers and Oscar Hammerstein II. Copyright © 1949 (Renewed) by Richard Rodgers and Oscar Hammerstein II. WILLIAMSON MUSIC owner of publication and allied rights throughout the world. International Copyright Secured. All rights Reserved. Reprinted with Permission.

"I Wanna Be Loved by You" by Bert Kalmar, Herbert Stothart, Harry Ruby © 1928 (Renewed) Warner Bros. Inc. Rights for Extended Renewal Term in U.S.A. controlled by Warner Bros. Inc., Harry Ruby Music and Edwin H. Morris & Company. All rights outside U.S.A. controlled by Warner Bros. Inc. All Rights reserved. Used by Permission. Warner Bros., Miami. FL. 33014.

Cover paintings and line drawings: Diane Way

Book design: Totino Busby Design Inc.   www.totino.com

Thanks! Lori Krupa!

Thank you, Mary Dawe, Mel, JQ, BTV, Annie Jannie, and Angie "I'm a Comma Person" Lemire

Photography: Connie Sawka

Printed and bound in Canada by Friesens

~ APRIL 28, 2010 ~ .

For Mom and Dad

TO: JOANNE!

WHO LOVES THIS

MOON!

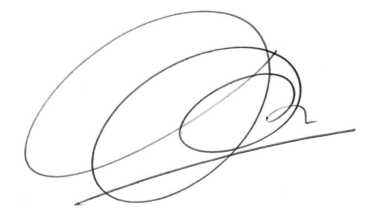

ON MOUNTAINTOP ROCK

– History is *we*, not *them* –

Contents

When I look into the corners of my mind for my childhood, the first thing I see is a back alley strewn with garbage and toppled trash cans – the bears are finished their nightly feast. It's a bright summer morning and I'm shouting my Tarzan yell. The sky is blue, the air is clean, and the mountains are resplendent; small, white fluffy clouds cling to their craggy tops.

Easter Sunday April 23/2000 At the top of Old Fort Point Hill

Jasper in the Canadian Rockies...

We had an apartment in Quebec City,

on avenue Saint-Geneviève, near the grand hotel Chateau Frontenac. The window at which I wrote every day faced a small park, and it became my habit at lunchtime to take my sandwiches outside and eat them beneath the trees, in dappled sunshine.

One particular day the park greeted me with music. It drifted happily through the treetops, mingling with the rattle-clip-clop of the old city's horse drawn carriages. Banners were being hung, stages were being built, and beyond the park along the boardwalk that looks to the river, juggling clowns practiced their funny faces. The great summer party was about to begin. Preparations were under way for the annual Festival d'été de Québec.

When I arrived at my usual spot with my lunch, there was a well-dressed, grey-haired woman sitting there. She was watching a small boy at play. The woman and I smiled and began talking. She told me proudly that she had been a schoolteacher and had lived within the fortressed walls of Old Quebec all her life. I told her with equal pride that I had been raised in the Rocky Mountains, in the town of Jasper, in Jasper National Park.

"Ah, les Rocheuses!" she said. "They are beautiful. I have been to Jasper twice. But I am sad to say I stayed only for one hour each time." She smiled at the child playing in the grass. "But the Rockies, they have been with me ever since."

"One hour?" I said, offering her a sandwich. "Why only one hour?"

"Merci." Her eyes sparkled as she gave half of the sandwich to the little boy. "Because of the train. That was more than 40 years ago, but I remember it so very clearly. I was a young girl – my final year at university. I made a summer visit to my aunt in Vancouver and took the train on my own both ways across our beautiful country, from Québec to British Columbia. Going west, the train stopped at Jasper in the middle of the night. The lights of the station were all I could see and I spoke to only one person, on the platform. But something about Jasper touched me that night. When I took the train back several weeks later, the journey was beautiful. It was a late summer afternoon – the last Saturday of the summer. I wanted to stay in the mountains forever, but I had to return to my classes at Laval. Since that day, I have never been back to Jasper."

"What do you recall from your short visit?" I asked.

"There was a beautiful pointed mountain standing guard above the town." The woman smiled. "I wanted to reach out and touch it."

"Pyramid Mountain."

"And the buildings were made of stone, smooth round stones, and I wanted to reach out and touch them, as well. And I remember the totem pole, painted with all the colours of the rainbow and carved with animals that reached up and touched the sky."

She looked down again at the child. "But so strange – I have another memory of Jasper. There were two children, a little boy and a little girl. They were playing at the foot of the totem pole, chasing each other round and round. The girl had a bandage on her forehead."

"They were playing tag?"

"Ah, oui. When I was a child we called it jouer á l'ours, playing at bears."

"At bears?"

"They were like little bears, those children, so natural and free. I sat on the stone wall that bordered the platform and watched them until the conductor shouted 'All aboard,' and then I stepped back onto the train and continued my journey home to Québec."

I stared at the woman. "1954," I said.

"Yes, '54. It was the last Saturday of the summer, a beautiful after-noon."

"The totem pole…." I looked up to the window of the apartment on avenue Saint-Geneviève to make certain I was not still sitting there at my typewriter and that this lunch and this woman were not just a dream. I touched the woman's hand. "Madame, you will not believe this, but I am certain – absolutely certain, that I was that little boy! I remember the day. Jenny and I, the last Saturday of the summer. The last train of the day, and someone else got on that train – someone else, made that journey."

"Someone of note," she said. "Yes. There was a crowd. It was only a matter of weeks before I read of that famous person's destination."

The woman opened her purse and took out a clean white handker-chief. "Because someone is famous does not always mean you think kindly of them. Over the years my thoughts have softened. I wish now I had said hello."

She wiped the little boy's face. "I have spent more than 40 years in the classroom. I have always impressed upon my students the impor-tance of remembering significant dates and time periods. But children find this so exceedingly dull."

Just then the music in the park grew louder, and a black and white harlequin clown staggered by on stilts, laughing and waving a long, red,

Quebec City

streaming strip of ribbon.

The retired schoolteacher continued to lecture in her soft thoughtful way.

"But as children travel through life they come in contact with the past; they meet people, they read, they watch movies and television. The dates they have been disciplined to remember become bench marks in their minds, and soon they start to cluster historic things around them; an era, a decade, a century – even a specific day. Those benchmarks become foundations upon which to build an understanding of life."

She placed the handkerchief back into her purse, and the clasp gave a soft click as she closed it. Then, to my amazement, she said, "I believe the journey, of which you speak, starting by train from Jasper, on that afternoon in 1954, led to an event that gave shape to the world we know today."

"I…I'm sure you're right," I said. "That event left an extraordinary image in many people's minds, an image that granted a lot."

She smiled. "You were lucky, my friend, to have lived in such a beautiful spot as Jasper National Park."

I gestured around me. "Vous aussi, Madame. Ville du Québec est l'une des plus belles cités du monde. C'est le coeur de l'histoire Canadienne."

"Ah, oui. L'histoire! History is also a journey." She stood and took the little boy's hand.

"And now, my grandson and I must continue our journey. Au revoir, mon ami. I have enjoyed talking with you."

I started to speak, but the woman and her grandson turned and walked away through the trees of the park.

For the next several weeks, I sat at my window on avenue Saint-Geneviève, and every day I took my sandwiches to the park, and every day I looked for the woman. As I did, my mind carried me back to the summer of 1954, when Jenny and I played tag beneath the totem pole and flew the kite from the top of Old Fort Point. That was the summer we searched for Henry House – the summer we found the battered tin box.

I did not see the woman again, but by the time the leaves in the small park had turned and the city of Québec was preparing once more for winter, I realized who she was.

With that, we gave up the apartment on Saint-Geneviève, and came home to the mountains. It was time to write of things that happened a long time ago. Time to search the corners of my mind for that last Saturday of the summer.

So, I am here again, looking down from this high spot, among these snow-capped peaks. I sit, as I do every year on this beautiful morning, and breathe in the fresh mountain air. Across the valley, I hear the whistle of a train, and I look towards my hometown, Jasper. The town is nestled against the hill, and above the hill stands Pyramid Mountain, a 9,000-foot stone giant, brown and black, and dusted in snow.

Come to this spot.

Climb the cliff and walk the dusty trail.

Stay in the sunshine, and watch for all the other living things.

When you reach the top, stand and look around. There are places we see every day and think nothing of, but to come here once, you'll recall it for a lifetime. The mountains, the river, the railway and the town, the people, the history, the blue sky itself – they all blend together into one beautiful watercolour softness. Jasper, beautiful Jasper.

Hans Christian Andersen once told a group of small children that to him mountains were the great folded wings of the earth. It's a lovely thought. But as we grow older, we examine the science of how the mountains were formed. Some say that hundreds of millions of years ago, during the gradual cooling of our planet, the outer crust became too large, and, in shrinking, certain parts folded to form the great highlands of the world.

But today on this high plateau, when the sky is blue and the air is scented with pine, at this spot where giant fingers can walk right up, step-by-step, to the sky, maybe these mountains really are the great folded wings of the earth, and maybe we can go back to that last Saturday of the summer. So, on this perfect morning, I let the great folded wings unfurl, and fly back to when I was a boy.

CHAPTER 1

BACK ALLEYS
AND BASEMENT WINDOWS

Jenny's mom practiced her singing early every morning as I laid in bed and tried not to listen. She always warmed up by singing a musical scale, the first note sounding with resonance and solemnity.

"Doe!" It came down through the ceiling, round and clear, and full of confidence.

"Ray!" And I imagined her upstairs by the piano, her eyes closed, her hands resting graciously upon her ample bosom.

"Me! Fah!" Quickly she moved through the rest of the notes, thinking, I'm sure, that if she sang them faster they would come out better. But they never did.

"Soe! La! Tee!"

Then with a high finish, full of crescendo and style, she gave forth with, "Doe!"

It was awful. Then she did it again, and again, and I never did get back to sleep. Eventually, Mr. Trotwood would shout, "Lovely, my dear! That's really lovely!" I could imagine him up there in his big chair, wearing the brown felt hat he never seemed to take off. "You're doing really well!" Then he'd smile kindly, shake his head, and go back to reading his scientific magazine. Mr. Trotwood liked reading scientific magazines. He said he learned a lot from them.

Mrs. Trotwood tried so hard to be a great singer. Interestingly enough, she always went up the scale, but never came back down. My dad said he didn't blame her, because it was probably hard to learn all those words backwards.

"Just the same," he noted, in his Glaswegian brogue, "ye have to admire Honoria's courage. She's brave and very sincere, an' it's great to at least try. Och! Music is grand! It separates us from the animals." Then he'd break into a chorus of "*I Belong to Glasgow. Dear ole Glasgee'toon...!*"

My dad admitted to having no ear for music and, therefore, felt he was more honest than most. "I must confess, Joan," he would say to Mom, "I know only two tunes. One is 'I Belong to Glasgow,' and the other – isn't!" Then he'd laugh and continue singing: "*Och!, but there's somethin' the matter wi' Glasgee, for it's goin' roond and roond!*"

The ironic thing about Mrs. Trotwood and her singing was that she was always telling Jenny and me not to make so much noise. On summer mornings, while we stood on Mountaintop Rock practising our back alley yells, Mrs. Trotwood would appear at her kitchen window and shout, "Will you please stop that racket!"

Then Jenny and I would jump onto our imaginary horses, slap our haunches, and gallop off down the alley.

In a town with no television and one radio station on the dial, Jenny and I spent most of the summer outdoors. We played "kick the can" and "punch the ice box," "red light/green light" and "Mother may I?" We played "Dinky toys" and we built forts. We went fishing and swimming, and we amused ourselves greatly with 'anti-anti-eye-over,' a game that involved throwing a baseball onto the roof of the house until an adult came out and yelled, "Stop that racket!"

On Saturdays, Jenny and I would go to the show. In the dark silvery world of the Chaba Theatre, we watched our great heroes. There were Superman and Batman, Tarzan and Robin Hood; there were cowpunchers and pirates, sea captains and soldiers, but the greatest champion of them all was our hero, cowboy Randolph Scott.

Every Saturday at the Chaba, a group of Missouri settlers or California homesteaders would trek across the U.S. looking for lost gold or buried treasure. Each week, without fail, they were attacked by yelling Indians or bad guys in black hats who needed a shave, and each week, without fail, Randolph Scott would jump on his horse and go for help. Just when things looked bleakest for the settlers, a bugle would sound in the nick of time, and hundreds of Hollywood extras – led by Randolph – would thunder across the screen, waving a U.S. flag. All the kids at the show would stand and cheer, as 'The End' appeared on the screen. Then the doors of the Chaba would open, and all the kids

would rush onto Connaught Drive and, blinking in the summer sun, mount their imaginary horses.

"I'll be Randolph Scott!" Jenny would shout.

"No, I'm gonna be Randolph Scott!" I would argue.

"OK. We'll both be Randolph Scott! Giddy up! Let's go!" And we would spend the rest of the day playing a game we called, quite simply, "guns."

While we played "guns," long elaborate dramas would unfold, and brave heroes would be wounded and stagger close to death. Somehow, though, by moaning and groaning and tugging at our chests, we always managed to shoot again.

You really needed a gun to play this game, so we made do with pointed index fingers, waggling thumbs, and imitation gun noises. Jenny and I each had our own identifying back alley yell and our own creative sound for the noise of a gun. My gun noise was made by a tight pursing of my lips, followed by a high-pitched hacking sound in the back of my throat. This was followed by:

"I gotcha! You're dead!"

"No, I'm not! You missed!"

And the shooting and shouting would go on till suppertime.

There was one thing about living in Jasper that made life a little different for Jenny and me. Every morning during the summer, it was our job to go out in the alley and find our own 45-gallon oil drum, stand it upright, and refill it with the garbage that had been scattered the night before. Residents of Jasper used metal oil drums with their tops taken off as trash cans. The family barrel was always kept outside the yard, up against the fence. In those days, there was no separating of paper and plastic, or potato peels and fish bone – everything was thrown into the barrel.

It was a rather inefficient method of garbage disposal, but a convenient method of feeding for black bears, who shuffled up and down the alley looking for delicacies. After dark, one would often hear the gong of a tipped barrel and then the barking of a local dog. In the distance, other dogs would join the chorus, and often at night as I fell asleep snuggled in my bed, the town would ring with the soft music of rolling barrels and barking dogs. And somewhere down the valley, the mountains would echo with the far-off sound of a whistling train.

I met Jenny Trotwood on a bright summer morning at Mountaintop Rock in the vacant lot next to our house on Patricia Street. Mountaintop Rock was on the very edge of the vacant lot. In fact, the huge grey stone jutted out a little into the back alley, and so served as a vantage point for looking both ways, up and down, into our world.

We called it Mountaintop Rock because it looked like the top of a mountain sticking out of the ground. There are still signs today of that rock vein running underground along that alley. Sometimes it goes from one side to the other, sometimes it pops up in a vegetable garden or pokes itself from beneath the roots of a pine tree. If you look carefully at the older homes in Jasper – the ones built in the '20s for a fast growing railway town – you'll see huge chunks of stone embedded in their foundations. When the basements were dug, the equipment used lacked the might to lift the boulders the glacier had left, and so concrete foundations were poured, leaving great stones sitting in cellars, or sticking out of basement walls. It became common to frame and gyproc around these massive stones, turning the area above into a storage space, or sleeping compartment. One of the most exciting things about coming to Canada for me was that I got to sleep in a hole in the wall. It was like a bunk bed with no bottom bunk – like sleeping on a mountain that came right up through the floor of my bedroom.

I walked down the alley to the vacant lot that first morning, and saw a girl with chestnut coloured hair. She was wearing a T-shirt, jeans, and high-top sneakers. She looked to be about my age. She sat crosslegged, on top of the big rock, with a small notebook and a pencil.

"Good morning!" she said, looking up. "I'm making a list of my very favourite lovely things." With the palm of her hand she flattened the notebook on the rock. I prepared to listen.

"I like it when you're in bed, and you make a cave under the covers, really close to your face...and you can look in there and pretend you're small." She sat up straight, and I nodded in agreement.

"And I like when water comes splashing into the bathtub and the bathroom fills up with steam." She looked at me and smiled. "And I like cool wind on a hot day, and climbing up, and looking back."

"Looking back? Where?"

"Oh, from up a tree, or from the top of a hill, or maybe, when you're in bed at night, looking back at what you did all day."

She thought for a moment and then continued to read: "I like the smell of laundry when it's hanging outside on the line, the taste of honey in your mouth – and stars that twinkle in a navy blue sky." She flattened the notebook once more and bit the end of her pencil. "And I like standing under a street light on a still winter night" – she was writing, now – "when millions of snowflakes are in the air, and you can pick one snowflake from all the rest...." She looked up into the sky. "And watch it come down, down, down...and catch it in your mouth." Then she stuck her tongue out and caught a snowflake that only she could see. "What are your favourite lovely things?"

"Mine? Well...I like fishing."

"Fishing?" The girl jumped down from the rock. "I like fishing, too! Who do you go with?"

"I've...I've never been fishing."

"Neither have I! But I could go with you!"

She grabbed my arm. "No, I'm sure I could! My mom and dad will say yes. You're my new friend from England. You and your mom and dad are going to live in our basement suite. Your dad is a cabinetmaker. He's here to help with the finishing touches on the new Jasper Park Lodge because the old one burned down. And your mom is a nice lady. I'm sure I can go fishing with you!" She tore out the page with her list of lovely things and put it into her pocket. "My name is Jenny, Jenny Trotwood!" She held out her hand.

"Edward, Edward Ferguson."

"I'm pleased to meet you!"

On that bright summer morning, I'd found a friend, and together we walked up the alley.

"My mom and dad and I have lived in Jasper for one year," said Jenny. "We came from Ottawa. It's the capital of Canada."

As we approached the house in which we both lived, there was a man going in the back gate. He was tall, with long arms, and he wore a blue uniform. Under one arm he carried a brown paper package.

"Sergeant Gumbrell!" shouted Jenny.

The man turned and saluted. Two rows of gold buttons glinted in the sunshine. "Hello, Jenny Trotwood!" His voice was deep, and it drifted across the fence in a singsong sort of way.

Jenny saluted back smartly and then whispered: "That's Sergeant Gumbrell. Don't you think he looks like a moose?"

"A moose?" I whispered. "What's a moose?"

The tall man had a small head, pointed ears, and a chin that went straight from his face to his chest. "I'm guessing," he shouted, "that this is our new friend from Scotland."

"I'm from England," I answered, "London, England. My dad is from Scotland. But my mom and I are from England."

"Ah, well then. Welcome! Welcome to you, and your mother and father. Welcome to Jasper!" He reached into a pocket of his uniform and pulled out a small white paper bag. "I am Magnus Gumbrell." Leaning over the fence, he smiled and held the paper bag towards us. "Humbug?"

Jenny reached in and pulled out a small brown candy. "Humbug!" she said. "Thank you, Sergeant Gumbrell."

He offered me a candy, too. I took it.

"We shall meet again," he said. "And when we do, I shall tell you of the time I sang with the great Bing Crosby!" As he turned and walked up the path, he began singing at the top of his voice: "*Happy talk, keep talkin' happy talk, talk about things you'd like to do. You gotta have a dream, if you don't have a dream, how you gonna have a dream come true?*"

The back door opened, and Mrs. Trotwood appeared.

"Good morning, Honoria," roared Sergeant Gumbrell. "It has arrived! The sheet music for *South Pacific*." He held high the brown paper package.

"They're practising," said Jenny, sucking on her candy, "for the great Broadway musical."

"I heard her practising this morning," I said, remembering being startled awake.

"The glee club is presenting *South Pacific* on the last Saturday of the summer at the school gymnasium. My mom and Sergeant Gumbrell are the big stars."

"Is he a soldier?"

"No, a policeman."

"A policeman?"

"He's Jasper's Chief of Police for the Canadian National Railways and for Jasper Park Lodge, too."

"For Jasper Park Lodge?"

"The Canadian National owns the Lodge. It's like a little village, with streets and shops and everything – and lots of tourists – so it has a policeman."

"My dad says famous people stay there."

"Kings and queens and movie stars. That's where Sergeant Gumbrell sang with Bing Crosby. He likes to tell people about that."

"He's a singer and a policeman?"

"He's Sergeant Gumbrell. President of the Jasper Glee Club and director of the Anglican Church choir. And he's police chief for the Canadian National Railways."

"Wow!" I said.

The sound of a living room piano drifted over the fence, and we listened until Mrs. Trotwood's high voice caught up: *"You've got to have a dream! If you don't have a dream! How you gonna have a dream come true!"*

"That's from *South Pacific*," Jenny said. "And there's going to be a volcano."

"A volcano?"

"Made of paper mâché, and it puffs out smoke made of dry ice."

Jenny headed across the alley. "Come on. I'll show you something."

"Is a moose like a mouse?" I asked as we walked.

"A moose?" Jenny laughed, putting her hand on my shoulder. "A moose is a lot bigger. I'll show you a picture, later."

Across the alley, there was another vacant lot with pine trees. In the middle of it was a shallow hole about 12 feet across, surfaced with yellow sand. "This is where I play Dinky toys," said Jenny, "and this is Mr. McKillop's three-quarter-ton."

Beside the sandpit was an old truck. It was blue, or had been before it earned its powdery patina. It had saucer headlights and a two-piece windshield, and on the back there was a rickety camper made of plumbers' pipe and grey canvas. The cab of the truck was huge.

"Mr. McKillop calls his truck Blue Lightning," said Jenny. "He drives it late at night."

"Where does he go?"

"I'm not sure. My mom says he's probably up to no good."

Next to the vacant lot, there was a garage made of brown wood. Snapdragons and pansies grew thick around its walls, and bees were busy beneath the eaves. On the roof of the garage a crooked stovepipe stood tipsy-like. Puffs of smoke drifted from it into a clear blue sky. The two garage doors that swung open to the alley were closed, but a gate in the hedge that ran along the alley was open. I followed Jenny through the gate, and we were welcomed by the sound of splashing water.

We were in a small back yard. To the right of the garage was a vegetable garden and a patch of lawn bordered in flowers. In the middle of the lawn was a small pond. From it, water gushed high into the air, splattering onto fat lily pads. The house was two stories with a peaked roof. It was brown, like the garage, and tacked onto the back of it was a screened-in porch.

"Wait!" said Jenny. She held her arms out dramatically, as if to hold me back. She placed a warning finger to her lips and pointed to the door in the side of the garage.

Painted on the door in green letters were the words:

Steel True
Blade Straight

and beside it was a wooden barrel full of old books with a sign on top that said:

Oak Barrel Book Shop.
Any Volume Purchased
For That Which You Have
In Your Pocket.

Jenny whispered, "Mr. McKillop's book barrel." She reached into her pocket and took out her list of lovely things.

Suddenly, a loud squawk came from above the door, and I jumped. On the roof of the garage, staring down through beady little eyes, was a big black crow. Its feathers were shiny and ruffled, and its claws scraped on the cedar shingles.

"*Smoky Bum!*" hissed Jenny.

"Smoky Bum?"

The crow cackled and hopped about, ripping up bits of shingle with its shiny black beak. "Caw! Caw!"

"His name is Smoky, but I call him Smoky Bum. He's Mr. McKillop's crow."

"Why do you call him Smoky Bum?"

"Because when the wood stove is lit in the garage, he sits on the chimney and warms himself."

Sure enough, the crow hopped onto the crooked stovepipe and put its tail feathers over the hole. When it started to bob up and down, puffs of smoke came out like Indian smoke signals.

"He can talk, too," said Jenny.

"Talk? What can he say?"

She looked at me earnestly. "He knows swear words."

"Swear words? Which ones?"

Her voice dropped lower. "He says 'hell's bells.'"

"Hell's bells? Why?"

"Because when he sits on the chimney, the smoke goes back down into the garage, then Mr. McKillop says bad things, and Smoky repeats whatever Mr. McKillop says."

"Who's Mr. McKillop?"

"He lives in the garage. My mom doesn't like me talking to him."

"Why?"

"She says he's – disputatious."

"What does that mean?"

"It's like cranky. But my dad says he's just a character. Mr. McKillop goes fishing all the time, and he really likes Sherlock Holmes."

"He goes fishing?"

"All the time. And the Blossom sisters live here in the Donald Duck house. They're really old, and they paint pictures of the mountains. The Blossom sisters are my friends."

"Why do you call it the Donald Duck house?"

"Because, look."

I stared in amazement. The two top windows were like eyes, and the roof of the porch, a beak. "Donald Duck. It looks just like Donald

Duck." Again the crow squawked as he bounced his bum over the stovepipe. "Why is Mr. McKillop so dispu...?"

"I don't know. He's just always arguing – especially with Sergeant Gumbrell. They're *always*...disputating."

"And Mr. McKillop owns the Oak Barrel Book Shop?"

Jenny nodded. "It's usually at the front of the house. He must be putting more books into it. He likes reading, and music, too. And sometimes strange voices come from his garage."

I shook my head at the wonder of these things. "Strange voices...."

But then, an angry voice leapt from behind the walls of the garage. "Hell's bells! Smoky! Ya beggar! Get yer bum off there!"

And on the chimney, Smoky waggled his tail feathers and flapped his wings. "Hell's bells! Hell's bells! Caw! Caw!"

The voice in the garage said 'hell's bells!' again, and Jenny whispered 'hell's bells' to me. She dropped her list of lovely things into the

barrel and grabbed an old book with a leather cover. Then, the two of us ran from the yard. For the rest of that glorious summer morning we said those delicious words to each other, over and over: "Hell's bells! Hell's bells! Hell's bells...."

Our back alley was a magic world. Jenny knew every picket fence and vacant lot, every hiding place and short cut. She conjured boulders into castles and turned groves of trees into paddocks for imaginary horses. Whether the air was spiced with sunshine, or splattering drops of rain made the neighbourhood smell of aspen and black poplar; whether rough winds blew to make drying laundry flap and dance, or long sweltering days turned to slow sticky honey, our wondrous alley, in all its many moods, was forever an enchanting place. I'm certain that summer itself lived there. But, for Jenny and me, there would be no place of mightier magic than the old brown garage where Smoky and Fraser McKillop lived.

CHAPTER 2

THE DARK EYES OF A STRANGER

That night there was a meeting of the Jasper Glee Club. So, all day Mrs. Trotwood bravely practiced her songs.

"*Some enchanted evening, you may see a stranger…*"

My mom, on tiptoes, peered through the window into the gathering dusk. "Such a lovely song," she said, her face close to the mosquito screen. "And it really *is* an enchanted evening – everything so soft and still. I think the mountains are going to sleep." She took off her apron. "And I'm all for going to the pictures."

Within minutes, the three of us were walking hand in hand down Connaught Avenue to the Chaba Theatre.

"Great!" said Dad. "A cowboy picture." We scrutinized the black and white photographs that showed highlights of the movie playing at the Chaba. I looked up and read aloud from the bright marquee: "*Thunder over the Plains!* Starring Randolph Scott. Hell's bells!"

Mom cuffed me over the head. "Edward! How dare you!" Her voice went very high. "Where did you learn to say that?"

"I…I heard it in the alley."

"Well, it's not nice!"

Chastened, I followed my parents into the theatre to watch Randolph Scott save the day.

After the movie, when the mountains were asleep, we returned to our basement suite. Outside, night had fallen, and across the valley the Rockies were slumbering silhouettes. Long black rows of saw-toothed peaks lay stark and jagged against a blue luminous sky. Stars twinkled above the town, and everything was still. But through the mosquito screen of our small, ground-level kitchen window, the dark eyes of a stranger were peering in.

My dad, one hand ceremoniously gripping a cast-iron skillet, the other holding a spatula in sceptre fashion, turned from the stove to address his family.

"Aye! An' now it's time for the illustrious chef, bearing with honour and humility the renowned mantle of virtues handed down to him through Scottish culinary history," – he raised the spatula – "holding high this emblem of power, I will now create the great, world famous Glasgow Bacon Sandwich." Rashers of frying bacon spat at him from the hot pan. "Och, there's nothin' like a good fry-up!"

Mom gave Dad her look and then pointed at me with the true authority. "But then, young man, it's B-E-D. Into your pyjamas, please. And tidy your room."

"Aw, Mom."

"Don't make me tell you again."

"But…."

"No *buts*! Into your pyjamas. And don't shove everything into the closet."

Dad flipped sputtering bacon. "Do what yer mother tells ye. Yer pal Jenny's already asleep. I see her light's out, up the stairs."

This wasn't true. Jenny's bedroom was the entire attic of the house, and I learned later that when my parents and I had returned from the movie, the click from the latch on the back gate had signalled her to turn her room to darkness. She had mistakenly thought that her mom was coming home from the glee club.

Like me, Jenny was not allowed to stay up late; but she loved to read, and with her dad in his chair with the *National Geographic*, and her mom out for the evening, she felt it safe to leave her bedside lamp on. She was reading the book she had bought that morning from the Oak Barrel Book Shop.

Later, when Jenny's mom really *did* get home, Jenny didn't hear the latch on the gate, and neither did the owner of the dark eyes that were staring so intently through our basement window.

As Mrs. Trotwood walked down the path beside her house, she looked up and sniffed with disapproval at the light from her daughter's window. At that exact moment, with her face turned to the heavens, Mrs. Trotwood felt something warm and soft strike her above the knees. In the basement suite we heard her anguished cry: "Help! Reg! Help!"

Mom and Dad and I ran outside and up the path. Jenny and her dad were coming down the other way.

"Honoria! Honoria! My dear!" cried Mr. Trotwood. He was still wearing his brown felt hat.

In the light cast from the basement window, we could see Mrs. Trotwood sprawled across the path. "Reg!" she cried. "It was lying there, across...." She pointed with a trembling hand. "A bear!"

We looked up, and there on the flimsy wire fence, hanging on with paws, claws and furry legs, was a frightened little black bear.

"A bear," stammered Mrs. Trotwood.

The fence wobbled and twisted, and the struggling bear cried out as it teetered amongst the Virginia creeper – one moment looking like it was going to drop back into the yard, the next like it was going to fall into the vacant lot.

"Do something!" shouted Mrs. Trotwood. "Do something!" And my dad held up his spatula into the night. The fence buckled violently and then sprang back with a great shaking of summer leaves. The bear thudded down into the vacant lot, and without stopping for a goodbye or I'm sorry, bound into the darkness of the back alley, dragging a long veil of shredded Virginia creeper.

"It was lying there!" said Mrs. Trotwood, holding her hands to her bosom and indicating with her eyes. "Lying there across the path. Its nose was against the window!"

Mr. Trotwood held his wife close. "Not to worry, Honoria. It was only a little bear – a cub."

"Reg! You are the assistant superintendent of Jasper National Park." She sniffed. "There should be no animals in *our* yard! That bear was looking through the basement window!"

My dad held his spatula behind his back, and Jenny hid her book beneath her arm. Mom patted Mrs. Trotwood's shoulder. "It's all right, Honoria. You've had a terrible shock. Let's go inside and have a cup of tea – and a bacon sandwich…."

Mrs. Trotwood's eyebrows drew together. "Bacon sandwich?" She squinted at my dad. "You were frying bacon? At night?" She sniffed

again and her voice reached the top of its scale. "With the window open?" She sputtered. "Are you trying to attract every wild animal in the park into our yard?"

Later that night, in my pyjamas, and falling asleep, I heard the distant gong of a tipped barrel and the far off barking of a neighbour's dog. I dreamt of bears and crows and strange voices from behind wooden walls; and, all in all, as I snuggled up on the mountain that ran right through my bedroom, I was happy to be living in Jasper, in the great country of Canada.

My dad never fried bacon with the window open, again.

Chapter 3

Whatever You Can Dream

Jenny was lost in the leafy world of the Blossom sisters' hedge. "Here's another one!" she shouted, and carefully withdrew her arm from the green prickly branches. "There's lots. Look!"

Across the back of her hand crawled a tiny red ladybug. She turned her palm and gently brushed it into a glass jar filled with fresh twigs and then held it up for me to see. "This is my bug jar. The Blossom sisters have the best ladybug hedge in the alley." She reached into her pocket and took out a metal lid that had been punched with nail holes and twisted it on. "And every day, at three-o'clock, they have toast and marmalade. Let's go!"

As we walked between the splashing fountain and the door that said *Steel True – Blade Straight*, I asked, "Why do you think Mr. McKillop argues with Sergeant Gumbrell?"

"My dad says Mr. McKillop doesn't like authority, and Sergeant Gumbrell is a policeman. But I've noticed Mr. McKillop never argues with my dad, and my dad has lots of authority."

"Why does he have it?"

"He's the assistant superintendent."

"Superintendent?"

"The superintendent is the big boss of the park, and my dad is the assistant superintendent. He's second in command for all of Jasper."

"So why doesn't Mr. McKillop argue with *him*?"

"Because my dad knows about stuff. He reads lots of books and scientific magazines."

"What kind of stuff?"

"He knows about plants and animals, and how things work, and about history."

"What history?"

"The history of Jasper."

"What is it?"

"What's what?"

"The history of Jasper?"

She placed the bug jar on the path and stood at attention. "Jasper National Park was created in 1907 to preserve a scenic mountainous area and its wildlife. It's located on the eastern slope of the Rocky Mountains, in the province of Alberta...." She was speaking like an actress in a play.

"The park encompasses 4,200 square miles, including the town of Jasper, the Athabasca Valley and the Columbia Icefields. Other attractions include animals such as bears, elk, moose, caribou, and cougars. Birds include eagles, hawks... and there are lots of trees and fish." She picked up the bug jar. "That's the history of Jasper. I learned it from my dad."

I nodded with appreciation and followed her up the steps and into the Blossom sisters' back porch. "My dad knows stuff, too," I said, as the screen door slammed behind us.

In the porch, the air was cool and fresh and smelled of spring flowers and freshly dug earth. We were now standing in front of a door that went into the house. To the right of the door, there was an old stand-up radio, and on either side, there were two armchairs that looked out to the back yard. Sitting on the radio were an empty flower vase and two teacups, each decorated with a picture of the new queen. Behind the radio, on the floor, there was an old typewriter. I bent down and tapped one of its keys.

Jenny lifted her hand to knock on the door. It opened suddenly and the rich smell of newly baked bread rushed out. A tall lady was smiling down at us.

"Hello, Jenny! Come in! Come in!"

The lady had white hair and wore a blue, flowery cotton dress. She had beautiful grey eyes, and her face looked very kind. Behind her, sitting at the kitchen table, was another lady with white hair. She, too, wore a flowery dress, but in pink, with a soft pink cardigan over top.

The lady at the door cried, "It's Jenny and our new friend. Hello, young man. Welcome! Welcome!"

I started to say "How do you do," but as she shook my hand, I couldn't take my eyes from the clock that hung above the sink. It was shaped like a cat. With each tick-tock of the clock, the black cat's tail swung back and forth, and back and forth, and its eyes looked from side to side. But even though it was afternoon, the little hand and the big hand both pointed straight up.

"Pleased to meet you," I said, staring at the cat.

"Your name is Edward, and my name is Kate, Kate Blossom; and this is my sister Pat." She turned to her sister. "Pat, this is our new friend, Edward. He's from England."

The lady at the table smiled faintly and whispered, "I let it go. I let it go." With both hands in her lap, she held tightly to a fold in her cardigan. With her thumbs, she stroked the fold as though she were shelling peas.

"He's from England, Pat. Where we're from. Where Queen Elizabeth is from, and the late King George."

"The queen...of England?"

"And she's our queen too, Pat. Don't forget. She's our queen, too."

Kate Blossom's face beamed. "Who would like toast and marmalade and a glass of cold milk?"

"Please," said Jenny.

I was looking again at the clock on the wall.

"I see you like our cat, Edward. He's still ticking, but I'm afraid his hands have stopped at lunchtime." Kate laughed. "Jenny, you get the milk from the fridge, and I'll make the toast." As Kate Blossom went to the counter, I noticed that she was limping and using a walking cane.

Everything in the Blossom sisters' kitchen was made of polished arborite and shiny chrome. On the walls there were framed pictures of mountains, all of them in watercolour.

"We painted them ourselves," said Kate. "Mountains are very strong and they can be dangerous, but they have a softness, too, don't you think?" She put butter and marmalade on the table. "There's Tekarra and Mount Edith Cavell. There's Old Fort Point, Pyramid, and Old Man. You see Old Man Mountain, Edward? It looks just like an Indian warrior lying asleep. He's wearing a beautiful head dress, full of feathers." She looked at her sister. "We've been painting for over 50 years, haven't we, Pat? We started when we were little girls, about your own age, Jenny."

Pat raised her hand in a curious way, like she was holding a brush. "We're painting...the sets for...." Her hand shook, and she put it back in her lap.

"For *South Pacific*. That's right, Pat. We're going to paint a beautiful desert island in the middle of the ocean. It's going to be a backdrop for one of the scenes." There was a touch of sadness in Kate's smile. "Pat and I have no talent for singing like Jenny's mom, but we can paint. And if everyone does their part, then Jasper will be a strong community. Have some more toast, Edward."

While Jenny and I ate toast and marmalade, Kate Blossom told us how she and her sister had come to Jasper.

"We came from England, like you, Edward. Our father was a member of the Northwest Mounted Police, in the city of Edmonton."

"A Mountie," asserted Jenny, "with a red jacket and everything."

"Very true, dear. And he came here to the Rockies on horseback, with a patrol in 1897. We were just children, your age, and when the patrol returned to Edmonton, Daddy told us all about the mountains and how beautiful they are."

"Did he have a gun?" I asked.

"He did, and he rode a horse, and in the old photographs he looks just like a cowboy. Constable Alfred Daisy Blossom of the Northwest Mounted Police." Kate spoke proudly. "Daisy was his nickname, but he was a big strong man, and he helped to keep law and order here in the west."

Pat's hands were still busy with the fold in her cardigan. "Daddy was...always searching," she said. "Always searching for...."

Kate took her sister's hand and held it gently. "Daddy was always searching for a new frontier, or a new adventure – always looking for a revelation. He used to say 'If you climb up every mountain and walk into every valley, one day you'll surprise the Great Creator at his work.'"

"The Great Creator," said Jenny. "Did your father ever find him?"

"I believe he did. Daddy loved Britain, and he loved the British Empire, and when the Boer War broke out in 1899, he left Edmonton to fight in South Africa. Mother was fond of Canada, too, but she was happy to take us girls back to England." Kate looked again at the water-colour mountains on the wall. "When we got back to England, Pat and I attended the famous Slade Art School in London, while our...."

"And you learned to paint," interrupted Jenny.

"We learned to paint, and..."

"Then you came back to Canada."

"No, not right away. When the war in Africa was over, Daddy returned to England, too, and took up life as a country gentleman. Our estate was in the county of Surrey, near the village of Hindhead. Then Daddy worked for the government." Kate's smile faltered. "He, he traded his cowboy hat for a topper."

"A topper?" I asked.

"A man's hat, Edward. Black and very tall – worn on formal occasions."

"What formal things did he do?" Jenny asked.

"Daddy was a remarkable mediator. He worked for the Foreign

Office at Whitehall." The smile was back on Kate's face. "When Pat and I were finished art school, we made a Grand Tour of Europe with our paint boxes and our easels. It was wonderful to see more of the world and make beautiful pictures of plants and animals."

"And *then* you came back to Canada?"

"We…did. Our parents stayed in England, but in 1910 we came back to Canada to see the mountains our daddy had told us of, and we stayed. We stayed right here in this beautiful valley. Here, in the middle of the eye of nature."

Kate's eyes now moved to the kitchen window. On the other side of the porch screen, bright water from the fountain sparkled against the green lawn.

"Mother and Daddy taught us to love the great outdoors. They encouraged us to see places and learn about things. 'Never be afraid to take a chance,' they used to say. 'You girls never be afraid to take a chance.' The wild west didn't scare our parents, and it didn't scare us, either."

"Daddy held his courage," said Pat. She was rocking gently back and forth, in her chair. "Daddy held his courage."

Kate was still staring at the fountain. "Our daddy used to say you could hold your courage in the palms of your cupped hands. He said courage is small, but it has power and magic, and if you pick it up with both hands and hold it right out in front of you, your fears will go away. Daddy believed that courage was wrapped up in genius. 'Whatever you can do, or dream you can do,' he would say, 'then do it!' Then he would stand straight and tall and shout:

> *Life is mostly froth and bubble!*
> *Two things stand like stone!*
> *Kindness in another's trouble!*
> *Courage in your own!*"

Kate smiled. "Then our dear Daddy would hold his head up high and say, 'Hah! Face up to trouble, and spit in its eye!'"

Jenny looked down and cupped her hands. "Did you and Pat hold your courage?"

"We did. When we first arrived in Jasper, the town was called Fitzhugh. There was nothing here then but pine trees and shacks and lots of round stones. We were living on the frontier."

Her face brightened. "And we were here in 1911 when the first train arrived. It was exciting, wasn't it, Pat? The huge locomotive came bashing and clanging into the siding, and you could hardly see for all the steam and smoke. The bells were ringing, and the pistons were crashing. The wheels were as big as me." She paused. "Have some more toast, Edward. And there's lots more milk."

Kate gripped her cane and stood up. "So, tell me, Jenny. Pat and I looked out the window yesterday when Smoky was making such a racket. What book did you buy from the Oak Barrel Book Shop?"

Jenny wiped her mouth with the back of her arm. "*The Complete Stories of Sherlock Holmes: Volume Two*. It's about a detective who's tall and has a nose like a hawk, and he's really smart. He learns about people just by looking at things, and he wears a hat like a baseball cap, but with a peak on the front and a peak on the back, and he smokes a pipe, and his best friend is a doctor."

"Oh, my!" said Kate.

"And the first story I read was about a horse...and a man gets murdered."

"Murdered! My goodness!"

"And the horse's name is..."

"Silver Blaze," said Pat. Her hands came up from her lap.

"That's right, Pat!" said Kate. "The horse's name is Silver Blaze."

"By Sir Arthur Conan Doyle." Pat reached for a piece of toast. "And I know who murdered the man." She spoke now with confidence. "Bet a nickel you'll never guess." She looked at me with a knowing smile and her eyes kindled. "You'll have to read it yourself. Sir Arthur Conan Doyle was a great writer."

"He was," said Kate. "And he was a wonderful man. He believed in honour and courage and doing things right. When he died in 1930, his wife, Lady Doyle, had special words carved on his gravestone."

"Steel True – Blade Straight," said Pat. She nibbled her toast, and then changed the conversation completely. "We have a friend coming to stay with us. A special friend, coming from...."

Kate touched Pat's arm. Pat hesitated. "I...I let it go. I...."

"Who *is* your friend?" asked Jenny.

"Oh!" laughed Kate, pointing out the window, "Smoky is making mud puddle soup."

We all turned to look. Beneath the sparkling water, Smoky the crow was jumping up and down in the pond. In his beak, he held a slice of bread. He shook it vigorously and threw it into the air. The water splashed all around him.

"He takes slices of bread from tipped garbage cans," said Jenny, "and the bread is so hard he can't eat it, so he softens it in the water."

Kate Blossom reached out and touched her sister's arm again. "Well, that was a lovely visit, wasn't it, Pat? And it is such a nice day."

"But, who's coming to stay with you?" asked Jenny.

"Oh, just a friend, coming for a few days."

Once more, Pat rocked gently back and forth. "The Indian people...." She stared at the top of the table. "The Indian people

believed...if you had your picture taken, the camera stole your soul."

Kate stood. "That's right, Pat, that's very true. Well, children, please say hello to your parents. We're going to invite your mothers for lunch very soon."

Jenny and I put our dishes into the sink, said thank you, and stepped again into the porch. Through the grey screen, I could see the fountain shimmering above the flowers and the lawn and across the alley, I noticed that the window of Jenny's bedroom looked down onto the roof of the old garage where Smoky the crow was now ripping apart a piece of wet bread. As we stepped down from the porch, I looked back to say thank you again and noticed that the vase on the stand-up radio was now full of fresh flowers. They were pansies and snapdragons.

"Pat always says 'I let it go'," whispered Jenny, as we walked along the path.

"What did she let go?"

"I don't know, but Kate is very worried about her because she can't remember things anymore. And my mom and dad say it's really sad because Pat was the one who always helped Kate because of her bad leg."

"But Pat remembered about the detective," I said, "and the Indians having their picture taken."

We were in the alley now, and Jenny was unscrewing the lid of her bug jar. "I wonder who's coming to visit?" she said. She turned the jar upside down under the hedge and shook it gently. Slowly all the ladybugs crawled back into their leafy world. "I was just going to keep them by my bed anyway," she said. "I can come and see them anytime."

"Who murdered the man in the story about the horse?"

Jenny smiled. "You'll have to read it yourself. Come on! Let's practice our yells." And we headed for Mountaintop Rock.

Back alley yells were important to Jenny and me; we were always practicing them.

"First you do your Tarzan yell," she would say; and I would open my mouth as wide as possible and let loose with *Ahhhhhhh! Eeeeeeeeee! Ahhhhhhhh! Eeeeee! Ahhhhhhhh...!* at the top of my lungs till my face turned red. My dad used to say it sounded like a donkey he heard once on a bicycle trip around Loch Lomond.

Then Jenny would cup her hands to her mouth and make a long series of throaty trills that echoed up and down the alley. Even today, when I hear a loon across a misty lake, the curtains of time open and I see Jenny; her head is tilted back as she gives her call to the mountains and the clear blue sky.

CHAPTER 4

INTRODUCING YOUNG WIGGINS

My mom stood at the back door and gave her own back alley yell: "Edward! Your breakfast is ready!" and I ran straight home.

The screen door slammed as I charged into the kitchen. Dad was already at the table with a bowl of porridge, and Mom was at the counter putting things into a cardboard box.

"I've heard about him," said Dad to Mom. "When did ye meet him?"

"Yesterday. He was walking up the lane with two buckets of black oil, and he smiled. I said good morning, and he said 'Top of the morning to you, ma'am, and I'll keep the rest of the day for myself.'"

Dad laughed. "Aye. That's him. Reg says he's a character."

Mom folded a white tablecloth and put it into the cardboard box. "And then he said, of all things, he was off to paint his garage with the oil."

Dad took a mouthful of porridge. "Aye. It gives his garage that lovely rustic look. He slaps it on, and the sun dries it to a beautiful golden brown."

Now Dad was washing his bowl in the sink. "A most resourceful chap, says Reg. Gets the oil from the Texaco after they've changed it in the cars, and uses it like house paint."

I sat down at the table. "Who are you talking about?"

Mom put a bowl of porridge in front of me, and I gave it my porridge look.

"Don't stare at it like that. It's good for you. Have you tidied your room yet?"

"Are you talking about Mr. McKillop, who has the crow?"

Dad was now heading for the door. "Aye, Fraser McKillop, across the lane. He's a great fisherman. Right ye are then, Joan. I'll be back in a wee while. I'm off to get the big surprise."

I looked up. "Surprise? What surprise?"

"Eat your Scottish penicillin," said Dad, "and ye'll find out."

Porridge was always a big deal at our house. My dad always called it Scottish penicillin, and Mom made sure we got our daily dose. Rather than eat it, sometimes I put it in my pocket. Slowly, while Mom's back was turned, I would gently lift the spoon away from the table and drop the stuff right in.

"Mom? What surprise is Dad getting?"

"Eat your porridge, Edward."

Minutes later, Dad was back. "It's here. Come. Look. It's a beauty!"

Mom smiled at me as she wiped her hands on a tea towel, and I scooped the last of the porridge into my mouth.

"What d'ye think?" said Dad. He stuck his chest out with pride.

There in the vacant lot next to Fraser McKillop's garage was a big, shiny, grey car.

"Our new motor!" said Mom, clapping her hands.

"Well, it's no exactly new, Joan. It's four years old."

"Nevertheless, it's lovely!"

It was a grey, two-door Chevrolet, all clean and sleek in a round, solid heavy sort of way.

"We're goin' for a drive," said Dad.

"I'll get the picnic hamper," said Mom happily as she ran inside to get the cardboard box.

"It's a great car, Dad!" I said, as I wandered to the other side to turn out my pockets.

So, we got into the Chevy and drove down the Jasper-Banff Highway, through the pine trees, and along the west bank of the Athabasca River. What a wonderful morning.

"Ye're goin' to see things you've never seen," said Dad. He pushed his shoulders back and gripped the wheel. "Look at those huge stones in the river. Can ye imagine the Indians in their birch bark canoes, diggin' their paddles into the swirlin' rapids? Can ye see the water splashin' up in their faces – their feathery bonnets streamin' in the wind? Oh, this is a grand country, Canada!"

At mile five, we drove up a big hill and looked across the valley to a long row of mountains called the Maligne Range. We crossed Portal Creek and the Astoria River and passed the road to Mount Edith Cavell. At the Meeting of the Waters we read the historic sign telling of the fur traders, and at Leach Lake we stopped and had sandwiches and a thermos of tea. The sides of the highway were covered with flowers. Beyond, in the cool of the pines, elk and deer grazed, and we caught a glimpse of two beavers swimming in a pond in the middle of a grassy meadow. Throughout that happy drive, we looked up and all around us in amazement at the snow covered peaks that loomed above.

About 25 miles from town, the Chevy carried us down a hill that swung gently to the left, and we stopped on a concrete bridge.

"Wait till ye see this!" said Dad. "Athabasca Falls."

Through the open window, I heard a distant rumble. Then as I stepped out, a fine mist touched my face.

"Stay close to your father, Edward."

I ran to the railing to peer over, and my head was filled with a deafening roar. An immense cascade of white water crashed over a huge broken cliff. It seemed as if the earth had cracked and shattered, leaving the rocky bed of the river broken and scattered. The force of the water threw columns of spray far above the trees, and I moved close to my dad before staring straight down. As the canyon's fierce voice came roaring up, Mom reached out to hold my hand.

Over the noise, Dad was now yelling in my ear, "This is an example of the great power of erosion. Mother Nature, in the course of untold ages, with rushin' water as her chief tool. It took eons to create these great cauldrons. Can ye imagine?"

Far below, milky foam swirled in great rock bowls, while whole trees, ripped clean of bark and branches, were trapped, forever swirling like sticks in an angry soup.

"Look there!" said Mom. She pointed into the grey, drizzly mist.

Just below, the ancient walls were wet and gleaming. Moss and ferns grew from cracks, and tiny bluebells swayed gently above the abyss. Further down in the darkness, trapped sunshine made rainbows that danced above the danger.

"Come on," said Dad, "let's get a closer look." We followed him carefully along a trail across the shoulder of the canyon.

Close by, on our left, water leaped wildly and plunged, forming a spectacular curtain over the monstrous rocks. The thought of what would happen to anyone who fell down there filled me with a giddy fear, and I reached out to steady myself on a rusty handrail, the only thing between me and the terrible chasm.

The air was now moist and trembling, and I kept my eyes straight ahead. Suddenly Dad stopped. At the highest point on the canyon, on the very edge where the water shot out, we saw a man. He was standing in a cluster of dripping pines and staring straight down. His lips moved, but his words were lost in the crashing water.

"Be careful, Tom," said Mom.

We walked cautiously into a chapel of trees and the roar of the canyon softened. Mom was holding my hand. The man still gazed over the edge, but now we could hear his voice. It was gruff, like it had been dragged through gravel.

"And there deep down in that dreadful cauldron of swirling water and seething foam," he paused, pointing into the canyon, "will lie for all time the most dangerous criminal." Suddenly the man stopped and turned towards us.

"Hello!" shouted my dad. "You're quotin' well, sir."

"Elementary," said the man. He looked at Dad with one eye half closed. "Elementary, my dear fellow!"

He was a handsome man about the same age as my dad. His face was chiseled and tanned, and he needed a shave. He looked like a bad guy in a movie, but with no black hat.

He continued, "Holmes did use the word *elementary*, y'know, in the story called 'The Crooked Man.'"

"Go on," said Dad: "It's a pleasure, indeed, to hear the work of Sir Arthur Conan Doyle."

The man reached out and shook Dad's hand. "Doyle was here in 1914. Stood right here. Said he wished he'd killed the Great Detective over the Athabasca Falls, rather than the Reichenbach."

Dad was smiling. "He probably couldn't have brought his hero back from this creaming, boiling pit of incalculable depth...."

The man lifted one finger into the air and finished my dad's sentence, "...which, brims over, and shoots the stream onward over its jagged lip!"

Dad laughed, and the man said, "You know your stuff, sir."

"I remember a wee bit," said Dad.

"And this is your good lady wife?" The man now turned to my mom. "We met in the alley, ma'am. How do you do?" He gave a short bow.

"My pleasure, again," said Mom.

"Are you enjoying these beautiful mountains?" the man asked. "They hold up the very blue floor of heaven, do they not?"

"They're lovely," said Mom, resting her arm on my shoulder. "And what are you doing out amongst them on this fine day?"

"Ah! I'm searching. Searching for that which is lost." He looked down at me. "And this is your boy, who I've seen in the alley. How do you do, young Wiggins? I'm Fraser McKillop."

"Hello," I said, and I shook his hand. "You're our neighbour, who lives...."

"In the small palace across the lane. Right you are! Pop in anytime, and I'll tell you some fish stories."

"Have you caught any big fish?" I asked.

"Big? I've caught 'em as big as you!"

My dad laughed again. "You're obviously a lover of stories, sir. We will visit, and we'll talk more of the Great Detective. It's a pleasure to meet you."

"You, too," said Fraser McKillop.

"Enjoy your search," said Mom. "I hope you find what you're looking for."

We left Fraser McKillop at the crest of the falls and returned along the path, steadying ourselves on the rusty rail. We looked back to see him, still there among the pines. White plumes sprayed up around him as tons of water continued to crash into the canyon.

At the car, I took one last look over the railing.

"Edward! Be careful!" said Mom.

Quickly I stooped to pick up a small stone and held it out. I opened my fingers and the stone drifted down in a long straight line until it vanished forever in the churning water.

I looked up, feeling dizzy. There, across the canyon in the trees, was Fraser McKillop's truck.

As we drove home, the sun dipped below Mount Edith Cavell, and a soft golden light filtered into the valley. I sat between my mom and dad, and the friendly road stretched out ahead.

"Did you think Mr. McKillop was scary, Dad?"

"Oh, I don't think he's scary. He's full of hearty bluff and honesty, and he's no afraid to speak his mind, but I wouldn't say he's scary. He might be a wee bit eccentric."

Mom laughed. "Honoria thinks he's a wee bit crazy." Then she added kindly, "He struck me as being somewhat of a proud man."

"What do you think he's looking for?" I asked. "Lost gold? Buried treasure?"

"Aye, could be," said Dad. "But he might already have found his gold in the quotations."

"What were those words?"

"He was quotin' the great writer Sir Arthur Conan Doyle, from a story called 'The Final Solution.' According to that yarn, Sir Arthur's Great Detective falls to his death over a perilous waterfall in Switzerland."

"Did Sir Arthur Conan Doyle push the Great Detective?"

Dad smiled. "Aye. Well ye might say that, seein' that Doyle was the author. But, no, the Great Detective falls while havin' a wrestlin' match with his adversary, the evil Professor Moriarty. It ends, as the story says, *'as it could hardly fail to, with the two of them reeling over the falls, locked in each others arms.'*"

"What's an adversary?"

"An adversary is an opponent, or an enemy."

"Like someone who argues with you all the time?"

"Aye, that would be an adversary."

I thought for a moment, listening to the sound of the Chevy cruising down the highway. "Dad, what's a mediator?"

"A mediator is someone who helps to settle a dispute."

"Like between two adversaries?"

"Aye, that's right."

"And Dad? Why did Mr. McKillop call me Wiggins?"

"Wiggins," said Mom, putting her arm around me, "was a little boy who lived in the streets of London. He was the leader of a gang of boys who helped the Great Detective solve crimes. The gang of boys was called the Baker Street Irregulars. That's where the Great Detective lived – on Baker Street."

"And the Great Detective is Sherlock Holmes," I said.

Suddenly the steady hum of the Chevy's wheels was interrupted by two loud beeps. Fraser McKillop's truck pulled up on our left-hand side.

"Blue Lightning!" I yelled.

Grey canvas flapped and fluttered in the wind as the truck swerved in front of us. Dad laughed and waved out the window. "It's McKillop's three-quarter-ton. And look at that!"

The truck seemed to be bouncing along the road ahead of us. Above it, Smoky the crow was dodging and darting, and dancing in the air.

CHAPTER 5

OF REAL HEROES AND LOST FORTS

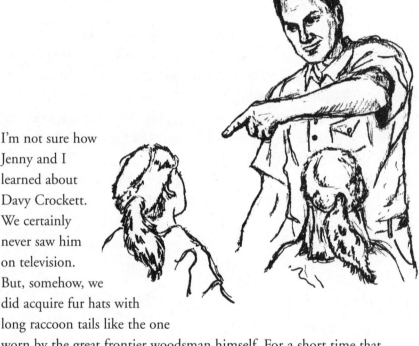

I'm not sure how
Jenny and I
learned about
Davy Crockett.
We certainly
never saw him
on television.
But, somehow, we
did acquire fur hats with
long raccoon tails like the one
worn by the great frontier woodsman himself. For a short time that
summer, our Davy Crockett hats were the greatest. We wore them day
and night – they were the centre of our being. We played Davy
Crockett, we talked and sang Davy Crockett, and, at the end of our
long Davy Crockett day, we left our furry hats on, and wore them to
bed. *Davy! Davy Crockett! King of the wild frontier!*

One Davy Crockett morning as Jenny and I walked down the alley, we saw Fraser McKillop painting his garage. He was sitting on a wooden chair, contentedly slopping black runny oil onto sun bleached wood. The oil drizzled and dripped down the outside of his living quarters, soaking itself into every parched board. Jenny and I approached cautiously.

"Good morning," said Jenny. "What are you doing?"

Fraser McKillop looked up. "Scratchin' my bum. What does it look like I'm doin'?"

"You're painting."

"Of course I'm painting." He went back to spreading the dark, shiny oil. There was silence as Jenny and I watched this irresistible exercise. Slop, slop went the brush. We stood wishing we too could splash and slop the stuff onto the dry thirsty walls.

"What's that you got on your heads?" asked Fraser McKillop.

"Davy Crockett hats," said Jenny.

"Davy Crockett?"

"He was King of the wild frontier."

"King of the frontier? The United States never had a king. What do you want to know about Davy Crockett for? You want Canadian history. History of your own. History of the mountains, and Jasper, and the Athabasca Valley. Not some fan-dangled, made-up, fancy stuff from Hollywood." He shoved the big black brush into the oil bucket. "Don't waste your emotions on Hollywood!"

"My dad says Canadian history is very interesting," replied Jenny.

"Well your dad is right. So I don't know why he lets you wear some foolish Davy Crockett hat."

I looked at Jenny and her bottom lip was sticking out, not in a sad way, but defiantly, like she wanted to punch Fraser McKillop in the nose.

"My dad knows lots about history. And he reads lots of books and scientific magazines. And he knows about animals...and birds and flowers...and fish!"

"He does, does he?" Fraser McKillop sputtered, and bits of black grit flew from his mouth. "Well, I'm sure, then, that your dad must know," he wiped his mouth with the back of his hand, "that the story of this country wasn't written in a history book." He reached into his shirt pocket and took out a small round can. "The story of this country was told in a ledger book. A big, fat, business ledger book." He took the top off the can, and with two fingers lifted out some stuff that looked like dirt. He tucked it neatly behind his bottom lip. "And it was the business of making what you guys are standing under. Hats."

His eyes were now fiery, and his bottom lip was sticking out, too. "But they were smarter lookin' hats than those dumb things you two are wearing."

My mouth was open at the thought of what he had put behind his lip, but Jenny fought on.

"These are Davy Crockett hats," she said with pride.

"Crockett Shmocket! You should have local heroes, like David Thompson and William Henry."

"Who are they?" I asked.

"Who are they? Who are they!" Fraser McKillop plopped the paint-brush back into the bucket. "Wait here." He went into the yard and disappeared through the door that said *Steel True – Blade Straight.*

"Should we stay?" I asked.

"He said wait here."

When he came back, Fraser McKillop had a bottle of beer and two bottles of Coca-Cola. He handed us each a Coca-Cola and sat down. He took a swig, and Jenny and I did the same, and we all wiped our mouths with the backs of our hands.

"There wouldn't be a Canada if those fancy fan-dangled Europeans hadn't wanted their fancy fur hats. And that's the truth." He picked up his brush and started painting the wall. "Trapping beavers caused the exploration of this country. At first, the fur traders took all the beavers from eastern Canada. Then they moved further and further west, and as they went, the rivers and streams ran out of beavers. They kept trapping until they got to what is now Alberta. Then the fur traders were stopped."

"Who stopped them?" asked Jenny.

Fraser McKillop took another swig of beer. "They were stopped by the great Rockies." He pointed his brush towards the snow-capped peaks, which now seemed just at the end of the alley.

"Then around 1800, there was a man named David Thompson. Now *there* was a great man!"

"Was he a hero?" I asked.

"He was a great hero. Greater than Batman. Greater than Tarzan."

"Greater than Tarzan?"

"Of course. David Thompson was a greater hero than…Randolph Scott!"

I looked incredulously at Jenny. "Greater than Randolph Scott?"

"You bet," said Fraser McKillop. He slapped more black oil on the wall, and it ran down in wavy rivulets. "Don't waste your emotions on Hollywood," he repeated and he rubbed the wall hard with his brush.

"What did David Thompson do?"

"What did he do? I'll tell you what he did. He unrolled the map of North America. That's what he did! He canoed and walked 55,000 miles. He was the greatest geographer in the world. A historian. A woodsman. A surveyor. He was a great author and a great storyteller. When Thompson told a tale around the campfire, you could hear the crack of the rifle or feel the snowflakes melt on your cheek. And he was a kind man; he didn't like killing beavers, so he spent his time exploring. He navigated rushing rivers and crossed sticky swamps and flooded streams. And he was a peacemaker, loved by white people and Indians alike. He could speak French, Italian, Spanish and four different Indian languages."

Fraser McKillop brandished the paintbrush like a sword. "Without David Thompson Canada would have no maps, and neither would the U.S. of A. There will be no greater hero…till they reach the stars!"

We were silent as the black, shiny oil soaked into the warm wood.

Jenny took another sip out of her bottle. "Mr. McKillop, how did David Thompson get across the mountains?"

"Call me Fraser. My friends call me Fraser. In the year 1811. In the coldest of cold winters, with over 20 feet of snow on the ground, when

Thompson and his men had hardly enough food to eat, Thompson's Indian guide, Thomas, found a way across the mountains. They followed what is now the Whirlpool River, up and over the Athabasca Pass. But before they started, they had to lighten their load. So they left a man named William Henry here in Jasper for the winter, to build a camp and look after the horses. Then, David Thompson, with 13 men and eight dog sleds, headed up the Athabasca Pass into a blinding snowstorm. It took seven months before they came down the western side to find the Pacific Ocean."

"Was Thomas the Indian guide a hero, too?" I asked.

"He was. Thomas was the only one who knew the way. He was a great hero."

"And William Henry?"

"William Henry spent the winter in the freezing cold waiting for David Thompson to come back. All winter, William Henry had to sleep on a bed of snow, and hang his bum over a cold log every time he wanted to go to the bathroom. He was a hero. You bet he was! And he built the great trading post, the old fort called Henry House."

"Old fort," I said. "Does it have a stockade? Do Indians attack it with flaming arrows?"

"No! And they never did. In fact, Henry House doesn't even exist any more. Worn away by time and the changing seasons."

"Oh," I said disappointedly. Then I asked, "Have you ever hung your bum over a log to go to the bathroom?"

He looked at me with one eye half closed. "Of course I have. When I go fishing. Everyone in Canada does. It's what gives our country its character. It's what makes a Canadian great."

"My dad says no one knows where the original Henry House was," said Jenny, briskly.

"Hah! That's because your dad doesn't know what I know. I've got a theory that's as clear as gin and as flawless as the Pope."

"How do you know?"

"I just know."

"Well, my dad…" she started stubbornly, but then considered for a moment. "Will you tell us?"

From the roof of the garage came a squawk, and Smoky the crow lifted himself into the air. The noise of his wings was like the spinning of a cowboy's lariat.

"You're a nosy crow!" yelled Fraser.

Smoky flapped faster until he landed on the top of a pine tree. "Nosy crow! Nosy crow! Caw! Caw!"

The distant bong of a chiming clock came from somewhere inside the garage. Fraser looked at his watch. "Eleven o'clock. Here, take over." He put the brush into Jenny's hand. "I'm off to the post office to check the mail. See you later." He turned and walked down the alley.

Jenny dipped the oily brush in the pot and then slapped it back and forth against the garage wall. "My dad says Fraser McKillop goes to the post office everyday."

I reached for the brush. "Can I have a turn?"

"And my dad says that nobody, but nobody, knows exactly where William Henry built the original Henry House."

She kept slapping the oily brush. "But maybe *we* can find out." She dipped the brush again into the bucket. "And if we do, maybe…." She looked at me like something wonderful was about to happen. "If we discover the location of Henry House, maybe we'll get our names printed in a magazine. A scientific magazine, like my dad reads. Edward, my dad would be so proud!"

She was slapping the garage wall even harder. "We've *got* to discover the location of Henry House." Oil was splashing all over the place. "They might even take our picture. Imagine. Our picture in a scientific magazine."

"Can I have a turn now?"

When I got home, my mom gave me her look. "*What* have you got all over you?"

"It's oil, Mom. Jenny and me painted Fraser McKillop's garage."

"Jenny and *I*, Edward. You must learn to speak properly. Oh, look! It's all over your nice Davy Crockett hat."

"I think I've worn it enough, anyway, Mom. Did you know the United States never had a king?"

"I did. Have you tidied your room?"

"Why do I…."

"Because when you grow up, you must be a neat and tidy person!"

"But, why…."

She interrupted. "Because if you develop good habits, you'll be able to get a good job and be happy."

"What are habits?"

Mom turned to Dad. "Tom?"

"Aye, well, habits," he paused, "are when ye do things… automatically."

"What does automatic mean?"

"Tidy yer room!"

CHAPTER 6

MARY SCHÄFFER'S SHOVEL

"I've seen
lots   of
bears in the
alley," said Jenny.
She used the toe of her
running shoe to drag wilted
lettuce into the tipped garbage can. Then she kicked in a pork chop
bone and an empty ketchup bottle. The bottle clattered as it hit thick
metal. "One night when my mom and I were walking home from the
show, we saw a bear's bum sticking out of a garbage can."

"What did the bear do?" I asked, pushing wet coffee grounds and
shredded newspaper with my foot.

"It kept eating garbage. It didn't even notice us."

"Do bears like garbage?"

"My dad said they must, because they eat it all the time, and it
keeps their coats shiny and black."

There was laughter from the other side of the fence. "I was joking, Jenny. Bears shouldn't eat garbage." Mr. Trotwood was shaking his head and smiling. He was holding what looked like a big wooden paddle with a long handle. "Jasper should have proper receptacles for refuse. It's not right for bears to eat out of garbage cans."

"Dad! Hi!"

"And," said Mr. Trotwood more sternly, "never presume a wild animal doesn't notice you. That's a very dangerous thing to do."

"Dad, would you be really proud if we discovered the original location of Henry House?"

"Jenny, I'm serious. Bears are very dangerous."

"But if we discovered where William Henry built his original fur cache, do you think we'd get our names in a scientific magazine?"

Mr. Trotwood was shaking his head again. "Well, I guess you would, but…."

"Why is Henry House so important, anyway?" I asked.

"What?"

"Why is the location of William Henry's Old Fort so important? If we find it, there won't be anything there."

Mr. Trotwood leaned the big paddle against the fence. "Local history is very important, Edward. The past is like a lamp that guides us into the future. The past tells us who we are, and what we are, and why we're different."

"Different from what?"

"Different from everybody and everything. The world is full of wonderfully different people and things, and we are all part of that wonderful world. History is *we*, not *them*. If you live in Jasper, you're part of Jasper's history."

Mr. Trotwood took off his hat, and for the first time I saw the top of his head. Except for some grey hair at the back and above his ears, he was completely bald.

"The fur traders are part of us, and we are part of them. If it were not for David Thompson and William Henry and others like them, we wouldn't be here."

"But the Old Fort won't be there."

"I don't deny that, Edward. When we think of historic structures, we think of mortar and stone, but the historic buildings of Jasper were mostly made of wood, and most of those no longer exist. The fur traders, the explorers, the railway builders, even the original sightseers, left precious little – sometimes only their stories – but a few touchable things do remain, and we should treasure them."

He picked up the wooden paddle again. "You see this shovel? It should be in a museum."

"That's a shovel?" asked Jenny.

"Hand carved, high in the mountains, from a fallen spruce tree."

Mr. Trotwood passed the shovel over the fence, and I held it with both hands. It was solid and heavy. "Why should it be in a museum?"

"Even the tourists are important to Jasper's history, Edward. The first tourist to visit Jasper National Park was a woman named Mary Schäffer. She was a talented artist, photographer and author. She was as much at home in a drawing room with the socially elite, as she was in a teepee with her friends the Stoney Indians."

Mr. Trotwood rested his elbows on the railing of the fence.

"In the beginning, Jasper was a national park with neither a railway nor a road, so it's hardly surprising that, at first, almost nobody came. But Mary Schäffer came just to look around. She travelled thousands of miles through mountainous country too rough for most. An Indian friend named Samson Beaver helped her find Maligne Lake, which became one of Jasper's greatest attractions. Mary Schäffer was the first non-native person to appreciate Maligne Lake. On her final trip in 1911, she actually mapped it."

"Like David Thompson," said Jenny. "Mary Schäffer made maps, and she had an Indian guide."

"That's right. Only this was 100 years later. When she reached the mountain pass into Maligne, in mid-June of 1911, the snow was up to her horse's belly. She had her trail crew fashion shovels from trees, and they cleared a path through the wet drifts. When she saw the shovels, Mary named the pass...."

"Shovel Pass!" declared Jenny.

"Was she a hero?" I asked, looking now more closely at the shovel.

"I think she was," said Mr. Trotwood, "but so were the men on her trail crew who guided her into the mountains."

"Did Mary get her name published in any scientific magazines?" Jenny asked.

"Lots of them, and she wrote books and had her art work and photography published, too."

"Would you be proud if we discovered the location of Henry House and had our names published in a scientific magazine?"

Mr. Trotwood opened the gate and stepped into the alley. He bent down and smiled at Jenny. "Jenny, I'll be proud of you even if you don't discover the location of Henry House."

He hugged her. Then he set the garbage can upright and put it back into place.

CHAPTER 7

A FAIR EXCHANGE

The next morning it was raining. I stood at the Trotwood's back door, draped in the plastic rain mac that had been bought for me in London and made wrinkled by its long journey in an old steamer trunk. It was noisy apparel with a strange smell. Its arms were too long so I could grow into them, and its matching floppy hat sat heavy on my ears.

"Hi, Mr. Trotwood. Can Jenny come out and play?"

"She's out already, Edward. I think at the Blossom sisters'."

"Thank you." And I ran down to the gate in the rain, splashing in the puddles with my gumboots.

Behind me I heard the soft notes of Mrs. Trotwood's piano as she greeted the morning with a song. *"Bali Ha'i will whisper on the wind of the sea."*

I had never seen inside Fraser's garage, but as I approached the door, I noticed it was open. I stood cautiously next to the Oak Barrel Book Shop.

"And this is a Royal Coachman, see? Lovely white wings, and a long tail of golden pheasant feathers."

I stepped closer. Inside, the garage was warm and dry and filled with soft light. I could hear the crackling of a fire.

"And this one is called Thunder and Lightning, wings of mallard feathers, and a body of orange hackle and gold tinsel. And here's a Mosquito, and a Dusty Miller, and this one is a Black Gnat."

I peered in further. The wallpaper was green and covered with sailing ships, and the wooden floor had been scrubbed and swept clean. In the middle of the floor, there was an oval carpet woven in many colours and around it sat wooden furniture that had been polished and rubbed to a shine. On Fraser's bed, there was a checkered quilt, and above it, carved in the headboard, was the face of a laughing dog – a hound dog, ready to leap, and jump up and lick my face. There were cups and saucers and plates and bowls, all in a row on a shelf, and along one wall, lined up like ready soldiers, were fishing creels and tackle boxes, bamboo rods and landing nets. Like everything in Fraser's garage, his tackle was clean and orderly.

"And this is my favourite. Careful now. It's sharp. That's the Silver Doctor. Blue wings and a body wrapped in tinsel. I always catch fish with that one."

"Always?" asked Jenny.

"Always." Fraser looked up from where he and Jenny were sitting at a wooden table. "Wiggins! Don't stand there like a drenched cat! Step into the parlor and take off yer slicker. And don't drip on my fancy rug. What do you have to say for yourself?"

I stood in the doorway in my gumboots and raincoat and looked around. From an old photograph on the wall, a man with a big grey moustache stared down at me. "Your garage," I paused, "is very neat and tidy."

Fraser straightened the oval carpet with his toe. "Neat and tidy? Of course it's neat and tidy!"

He helped me off with my raincoat and hung it on a coat peg next to the door.

"You can't just throw your things around. You start leavin' your clothes on the floor and you'll get spiders in your underpants."

"Spiders?"

"Of course, spiders! If you don't pick up your things and fold them properly, your underpants will be full of spiders."

I screwed up my face. "Did you ever have spiders in your underpants?"

"Once, when I was a boy. But never again. If you're neat and tidy, it'll never happen, and then you'll have a neat and tidy mind, too. Like Sherlock Holmes." He took a handful of firewood from a box on the floor and threw it into the firebox of the stove. The flames crackled, again. "Then you'll be able to solve great mysteries by using the power of deduction."

I shoved my hands into my pockets while I thought more about the spiders.

"Deduction?" asked Jenny.

"When you deduct something, you take it away. That's what deduction means, to subtract or take away. Sherlock Holmes said *when you eliminate the impossible, whatever remains, however improbable, must be the truth*. With the art of deduction, you can figure out lots of things."

"Like what?" asked Jenny.

Fraser fixed his eye on me. "Well, my powers of deductive reasoning tell me that Wiggins," he rubbed his chin with his fingers, and the stubble of his beard made a soft scratching sound, "Wiggins, this morning had porridge for breakfast."

I reached even deeper into my pockets. "How did you know that?"

"Simplicity itself," said Fraser. "You dribbled oatmeal down your shirt. Hah!" He laughed and slapped his knee. "But you understand the significance; never judge anything till you know all the facts."

"Maybe we could use the power of deduction to discover the location of Henry House." Jenny was still thinking about getting her name into a scientific magazine. "If we look in all the places that it might be, and it's not there, then the place we haven't looked is where it's at."

"I don't need deductive reasoning to figure that out," said Fraser. "I know where William Henry built his house." He dug into his shirt pocket and took out the little can of stuff that looked like dirt.

"Where?" asked Jenny.

"Now tell me, Wiggins," said Fraser, "you're from England, are you not?"

"I am."

"Ah, yes! Victorian England. Where the Great Detective lived." He tapped the top of the little can with two fingers and then took off the lid.

"Victorian England, fat with the fruits of her achievements, but strong and daring still with the spirit of imperial adventure. The seas pounding, the wind sweeping across her moors."

He thought for a moment. "I'd like to gravitate to London, that great cesspool," he stuck his fingers into the can and lifted out some of the black stuff, "into which all the loungers and idlers of the Empire are irresistibly drained." And then he neatly tucked it behind his bottom lip.

"I'd like to be free as air in London, or as free as an income of eleven shillings and sixpence a day will permit." He smiled down at Jenny and me, his bottom lip puffing out. "That's a quotation from Sherlock Holmes, by the great Sir Arthur Conan Doyle."

Jenny stared at him in amazement. "What is that stuff?"

He touched his hand to his shirt pocket. "Snoose."

Jenny, thinking this gesture some sort of signal or secret sign, placed her hand across her heart. "Snoose!" she answered and then looked at me, her eyes wide with questions.

Not knowing what else to do, I followed suit. "Snoose!" I said crossing my heart and giving a quick bow.

Fraser stared at us. "Well, whatever. Baccy's not good for you, and don't you be tryin' it!" He threw his attention back to England.

"So, Wiggins, have you walked down the Pall Mall? Or strolled the Strand? Have you been to Baker Street, where Holmes and Watson lived? Where the Great Detective solved all his famous criminal cases?"

"I don't think so."

"Maybe you've visited the Diogenes Club?"

"No. I…."

"Have you been to Whitehall, or the Foreign Office?" He leaned forward slightly. "That's where all the spies are, you know."

"Spies?" I said with heightened interest. "I don't think I've ever been *there*."

"Ah, well, not to worry." Fraser looked around the room. "What'll we do now?" He picked up a small, silver fishing reel and handed it to Jenny. "What do you think of that?"

"I'll bet you've caught lots of fish with this." She tapped the reel's ebony handle with her finger, and the oiled mechanism whirred. Yards of fishing line squirted to the floor in a black heap at Fraser's feet.

"Well, maybe we've seen enough of my domestic arrangements." He turned the reel's handle quickly and the line shot back into its case. "Let's do something else." He went to the big doors that opened to the alley, and swung them wide. Then he threw open his arms and took a deep breath. "Fresh mountain air!"

The rain now fell in silver sheets. Through the garage doors the alley was like a movie screen. We pulled chairs up to where the rain could not hit us, and we sat; and as the morning went by, Fraser told stories about how the mountains got their names, and about fishing in the high alpine lakes. He told us of the great detective Sherlock Holmes and his creator Sir Arthur Conan Doyle. And he told us again about David Thompson and all the characters who had explored and conquered the Rocky Mountains. And as we listened on that wet summer morning, we watched as all of Fraser's heroes marched up and down the alley, across the silver screen.

But at lunchtime, when the sun came out and the puddles started to shine, when Jenny asked Fraser to tell us more about William Henry and where he had built his original fur depot, Fraser looked at his watch and said, "Ah well, maybe that's for another day." He went to a marble-topped washstand, and, from behind a china jug decorated with flowers, picked up two books.

"Here, Wiggins. This one's for you."

It was old and tattered, and its blue cover wore the stain of a perfect circle from some forgotten bottle or glass. But its title was clear and it was printed in gold, *A Boy's Guide to Fishing*.

"And, Jenny, you'll need this."

Jenny examined the book in her hand. It was leather bound like the one she had bought from the Oak Barrel Book Shop. "*The Complete Stories of Sherlock Holmes: Volume One*. Thank you, Fraser."

"A fair exchange," he said, and he pulled Jenny's list of lovely things from his shirt pocket. "If ever I get to feeling sorry for myself, I can pull out this list and realize what a lucky guy I am." He put the list back into his shirt pocket and patted it. "I'm always going to protect this," he said with a big smile.

I reached again into my pockets. "I should give you something for this book." But all I had were dried up flakes of oatmeal.

"That's OK, Wiggins. One day you'll do something nice for me." With that, Fraser turned and headed down the alley to the post office.

"Fraser!" yelled Jenny. "Will you show us where Henry House is?"

He kept walking. "One day I will." But he didn't look back.

Jenny took out her notebook and pencil and made some notes.

CHAPTER 8

AN INVITATION TO DANCE

I was helping my dad and Mr. Trotwood rake deer droppings from the front lawn.

"Oh, aye," said Dad. "It's a grand hotel, the Jasper Park Lodge. In the main building, there's a huge stone fireplace. An' hangin' from the top of it, way up in the air, there's a buffalo's head. And the whole place has wall-to-wall carpet, and big windows, and a grand view of the mountains and Lac Beauvert."

I held open a canvas sack, and with one quick sweep of the rake, Dad sent in a pile of shiny black pellets and dried-up grass.

"Darn deer," said Mr. Trotwood disapprovingly. He tilted his hat back on his head. "All the flowers, gone!"

"Aye. They've had their breakfast. Two rows of snap dragons and a bed of pansies."

Across Patricia Street, three young mule deer were munching grass along a neighbour's fence.

"I've an invitation for ye, Reg. The Lodge is havin' a party the

Saturday after next, a dinner-dance for all the workers who helped with the rebuildin'. Joan and I were wonderin', would you and Honoria like to join us?"

"I'm sure we would," said Mr. Trotwood. "Actually Honoria will be singing at that party with the glee club. It's a warm-up for their big performance. An evening at the Lodge sounds great. I imagine it's a dress up affair."

"Aye, you've to wear a tie and everythin'. Cocktails at six and a live orchestra."

"That's the Lodge for you. Very fancy. The last big do we went to, all the movie stars were there. Honoria did the foxtrot with Robert Mitchum." Mr. Trotwood lifted the canvas sack onto his shoulder. "That was last summer, when they were filming *River of No Return*."

I followed the two of them to the garbage can in the back alley.

"And ye know, Reg," said Dad, "in the dinin' room of the Lodge, right in the *middle* of the dinin' room, mind ye, right there, among the starched, white tablecloths and the fancy silver, there's a grand fountain and a big trout pond. Enormous trout, as long as yer arm, swimmin' round like slow torpedoes. And there, eatin' their fancy meals, amidst the clink of fine china and the music of a string quartet, are all the swanky tourists. And – can ye imagine? – there, beside them, all those massive trout. Oh, aye. It's a grand place, the Jasper Park Lodge."

Mr. Trotwood tipped the sack, and deer pellets and dry grass fell into the oil drum. He coughed, waving a hand in front of his face. "Darn deer!"

"Good morning," announced a deep voice. "I see the deer have left their calling card."

Sergeant Gumbrell, in his blue uniform with shiny buttons, was about to go into our yard. He carried a pile of sheet music.

"Morning, Magnus," said Mr. Trotwood. "Yes. They jumped the fence last night."

"Higher fences," Sergeant Gumbrell said. "We need higher fences." He reached into his pocket and pulled out the small paper bag. "Humbug?" he said, bowing in my direction.

"Humbug!" I said, reaching into the bag.

My dad frowned. "What else do ye say, Edward?"

"Thank you," I said, sucking on the candy. "Thank you very much."

"Have you met Tom Ferguson, Magnus?" said Mr. Trotwood.

"How do you do, sir?" Sergeant Gumbrell shook my Dad's hand. "I've heard of you and of the fine job you are doing at the Lodge."

"Kind of ye to say," said my dad.

"We were just discussing the Lodge and the big party, Magnus."

"Ah. The dinner dance. Guaranteed to be a fine evening. Dancing on the shores of Lac Beauvert to the up-tempo sounds of the Frank Darlow Orchestra. I, myself, shall be there in my capacity as Chief of Police and, as well, shall lead the glee club in a sampling of tunes from our upcoming production." Sergeant Gumbrell patted the pile of sheet music under his arm and started to sing, "*I'm just a cockeyed optimist.*"

"When is the grand performance?" asked Dad.

"On Labour Day weekend. The last Saturday of the summer." His chest puffed out, and the gold buttons on his jacket jumped. "September 4th, at the Jasper Elementary School gymnasium. *South Pacific* will open the curtain on another season of culture and refinement here in our small community. I'm certain the whole town will attend." He opened the gate. "And so, farewell, my friends. When we meet again, I will tell you of the time I sang with the great Bing Crosby. Till then, good luck with your efforts to redirect the droppings of the mule deer."

Then we heard another voice. "A few deer turds won't hurt ya, Gumbrell! I'd rather sweep deer turds than hear you tell us, again, about tryin' to sing with Bing Crosby."

Sergeant Gumbrell's face came up like thunder. "You!" he shouted. "McKillop, you...nitwit!" The gate slammed and Sergeant Gumbrell stomped up the path.

"Morning, Fraser," said my dad.

"Morning, Tom. How are you?" Fraser was smiling. "Been frying any bacon lately? Hah! One of these nights you'll find a grizzly growlin' at your window. And Reg. Have you figured out where Henry House is?"

"Not yet, Fraser. Should we call in the Great Detective?"

"I don't need Sherlock Holmes for that." Fraser walked over to the vacant lot and thumped his fist on Blue Lightning's fender. "I know where Henry House is." Dust floated in the air as he looked under the canvas canopy. "I could take you there tomorrow!" He got in behind the wheel, and Blue Lightning's motor growled and then roared to life.

"He's a good chap, really," said Mr. Trotwood. "Goes for one glass every day, down to the hotel or over to the Moose's Nook at the Lodge."

"What does he do for a livin'?" Dad asked.

"Well, till a few years back, he was a miner up in the Coal Branch. But when the steam engines converted to diesel, they started closing the mines."

As Blue Lightning pulled into the alley, Fraser stuck his head out the window. "In the words of Sherlock Holmes, 'It's my business to know what other people don't know.'" He laughed and put his foot on the gas, as bits of yellow sand fell at our feet.

"Back tires look a little low, Fraser," shouted Mr. Trotwood.

"You just keep lookin' for Henry House, Reg!" Blue Lightning rumbled slowly down the alley.

Jenny now rushed down the path from the house. "Did Fraser and Sergeant Gumbrell have another argument? Sergeant Gumbrell says Fraser is a nitwit, and Mom says Fraser is just jealous of Sergeant Gumbrell. She says Fraser sits in his garage all day and talks to himself, and that Sergeant Gumbrell should follow Fraser one night and find out where he goes."

Mr. Trotwood folded the canvas sack. "Oh, I think McKillop just likes to get out on those mountain lakes before the sun comes up."

"Sunrise on a mountain lake," pondered my dad, "must be beautiful. By the way, Reg, what's the difference between a grizzly and a black bear?"

"Well, grizzlies are considered more dangerous. And they're a lot bigger. They usually have yellowish brown fur, with black on their spine and legs. You'd know one if you saw it – very small eyes and a flat face."

Dad and Mr. Trotwood headed up the path to the house.

"The moose's nook?" I asked Jenny. "What is that?"

She looked at me knowingly. "The Moose's Nook is a place where they drink beer." We watched as Blue Lightning disappeared down the alley. "But, I wonder where Fraser does go every night?" Out came Jenny's notebook and her pencil. "And I wonder why he's jealous of Sergeant Gumbrell?"

The next morning, I was dragging all my Dinky toys out from under my bed. From the kitchen I heard my mom's voice.

"Oh no, Tom. Aunt Edie thinks we live in a box!"

"A box?" said Dad. He was at the top of a stepladder, probably thinking about knocking out a wall. Dad was always knocking out walls or moving doors. He always left things better than he found them.

"A box, Tom!" Mom was holding a blue airmail letter. There were tears in her eyes. "When I last wrote to England, I told them Jasper was a railway town. Aunt Edie took that thought and combined it with our address, which is a box number, and now she thinks we live in some sort of packing crate by the railway tracks." Mom's voice was full of grief. "Oh, no!"

Dad laughed. "Aye, true enough, there's no box numbers in the old country."

"But, Tom listen!" The thin blue paper shook in Mom's hands as she read. "I am sitting here, Joan, my eyes wet with tears, thinking of you and Tom, and little Edward, and your sad situation. God bless you. I pray every night things will get better. You are so far from home. Love from all of us in Great Britain. Aunt Edie."

Mom pulled a hanky out of her sleeve and wiped her eyes.

Dad was down the ladder. He took Mom in his arms. "Oh, not to worry, Joan. How can ye tell them about Jasper? The mountains, the lakes, the rivers. They wouldn't understand."

"The other day," said Mom, "I wrote, trying to tell them about the town, and the wonderful people, the streets and the flowers, and the beautiful buildings. I just can't put it into words."

"Nobody can!" said Dad.

"I tried to tell them about the dance we're going to at the Lodge and about how we'll be waltzing beneath a white mountain on the shores of a beautiful lake. I couldn't do it justice. I can hardly believe it myself."

"Och! You can't describe those things with words." Dad started waltzing Mom around the kitchen "How could ye describe the beautiful green of Lac Beauvert? It's like summer sunshine, fallen from a blue sky, held forever floatin' within the secret of its own beauty. Ye couldn't describe that with words!"

Mom's head was on Dad's shoulder. She started to smile. "I must write that down."

Now they were whirling around the kitchen. "Och! Never mind dancin' on the shores of Lac Beauvert. If they could only see us now."

Mom was laughing. She kissed Dad's cheek and then pushed him away. "I don't have time for this, right now." She was smiling, but then looked serious, as she returned to the kitchen table. "I will not be happy till I know that my family in England understand – *we do not live in box!*" She sat down at the table with a pen and paper.

Chapter 9

A Very Important Letter

"You see, Edward? Way up there! That's the grizzly bear with her two cubs. And there's a frog, and a big bull with horns, and at the very top, the Raven with his beak sticking out."

Jenny and I were standing beneath the totem pole at the train station. It was two days before our parents were to attend the big dance at the Lodge. We were actually on our way to the post office because my mom was anxiously awaiting another letter from Aunt Edie.

Jenny kept staring straight up. "For each animal, there's an Indian story. The great Raven is half bird and half God, and when...."

"It came to town in 1919," thundered a voice behind us.

We turned to see Sergeant Gumbrell, hands on his hips, legs astride.

"The totem pole rolled in on a rainy night. All 75 feet of it, strapped to the top of a railway flat car. What a sight it must have been," he said gloriously. "Its huge beak pointing straight up, its eyes staring into a dark wet sky."

Like a gunslinger, Sergeant Gumbrell used both hands to grip the leather belt that strapped his tunic. "This totem stood for over one hundred years as a living tree in the forests of the Queen Charlotte Islands, and then a great Haida chief chopped it down and carved into its trunk the spirits of supernatural animals. Then, here," Sergeant Gumbrell stamped his foot, "at the Canadian National Railway station, its base was sunk nine feet into the stony ground. It has stood since, towering above our beautiful town." He sighed with satisfaction as he stared straight up.

"The Raven – " he continued.

" – is half bird and half God," Jenny interrupted, "and when the Great Flood covered the earth, he took his mother into his arms and flew her up into the air, and pierced a big hole in the sky with his beak, and all the water ran out, and then the earth was dry again. And now the Raven sits up there just staring across at Old Fort Point." She gestured with her arm beyond the tracks. "Old Fort Point is that big hill, over there, below Tekarra Mountain."

A mile and a half across the valley, a large promontory lifted itself in two huge humps, one above the other. "Like a hill giving another hill a piggyback ride," I said.

"It's easy to walk up," said Jenny. "From the top of Old Fort Point you can see the whole valley and all the mountains. And on both sides, there are really steep cliffs."

From beyond the red gabled roof of the train station came the whistle of a locomotive – two long blasts, then a short, then a long.

"The Trans Continental," said Jenny. "In the west yard."

With a long continuous blast, the giant diesel chugged alongside the platform. Gliding behind, came a chain of olive-coloured coaches. They crouched above the rails like great green panthers, thick oil gleaming on their steel axles.

Sergeant Gumbrell stood at attention.

"Are you waiting for someone?" asked Jenny.

There was a pause. "I am...for a friend."

"A special friend?"

He stood tall, taking his official stance, and said, "I hope so.

Maybe, on this train."

"Where's your friend coming from?"

"From Vancouver. She's been visiting relations." His eyes moved from window to window as the coaches passed.

"Is your friend going to stay in Jasper?"

"I hope so. We met earlier this summer, here, late at night. But I intend to…"

The wheels of the train screeched as it came to a halt on the shiny tracks. Porters jumped from vestibules to lower steps and help passengers down. Soon the platform was crowded with people. Sergeant Gumbrell, his hands behind his back, strolled searching for a face.

Without warning, Jenny slapped my shoulder. "Gotcha last!" She darted to the other side of the totem pole.

I chased her around the pole, but she was quick; soon our heads were bobbing back and forth on either side.

"You're it!" she yelled, and we played tag until we were both out of breath. Then we flopped on our backs on the grass beneath all the mythical animals.

"All aboard!" shouted the conductor, and now the platform was bare, but for one person standing at attention. With a long blast of steam, the wheels started turning – clickety-clack, clickety-clack – as the train pulled away from the station. The Trans Continental was now just a dot at the far end of the east yard.

"Maybe your friend will be on the next train," said Jenny.

"Maybe," said Sergeant Gumbrell. "Maybe tomorrow she'll come through on her way back to Québec."

He reached into his pocket and took out the white paper bag. He held it toward us, but said nothing. We both reached in and took a humbug.

"Thank you, Sergeant Gumbrell."

"You're welcome," he said.

"Poor Sergeant Gumbrell," Jenny said, as he strode down the platform.

From the other side of Connaught Drive came the long wail of the

fire hall siren. It blew everyday at noon to signal the lunch hour. Jenny and I ran across Connaught Drive, jumped over a flower bed, and crossed the lawn in front of a beautiful old building made of smooth round stones.

"This is where Jasper's first superintendent lived," she said. "He was from England, like you, Edward. His name was Colonel Rogers, and he called this building the Boulders. But now this building is the information centre where you find out about things."

As we walked past the Boulders, I placed my hand on a smooth round stone. It was cold and hard, and it felt good when I patted it with my palm. Then I followed Jenny across Patricia Street, up the steps and into the post office.

"What happened to the Raven's mother?" I asked.

The room we were in had a wall lined with small silver doors. Row upon row, near ceiling to floor, each door had a keyhole and a neat black number.

"The spirit of the Raven's mother still lives in Jasper. Seven-three-four. Seven-three-five." Jenny was counting numbers on doors. "Seven three-six! Here's your box, Edward."

I took the shiny key my mom had given me from my pocket and opened the door. There it was – a blue airmail letter from Aunt Edie, the one Mom was so anxious to read. I stuffed it into my pocket as Jenny took letters from her box.

"My mom will be happy now," I said.

As we headed home along Patricia Street, we came to a big brick building called the Athabasca Hotel. "This is where Fraser goes every day," said Jenny. A big sign on the door read *Gentlemen Only.*

"The Baker Street Irregulars!" shouted a voice. We turned, and there was Fraser.

"You two are a long way from home."

"We checked the mail, like you do everyday," Jenny said.

"Ah, the mail. Well, I've been to the post office already. I'm just goin' in here to, uh…," he paused, "see a man about a dog."

"A dog?" said Jenny joyously. "Are you getting a dog?"

"I might. You never know." Fraser opened the door and we peered into a dimly lit, smoky room. We saw an elk head on the wall and a big snarling wolverine above a bar lined with bottles.

Suddenly Fraser blurted. "Gumbrell!" Jenny and I jumped. "In the gum machine."

Behind us on the street, a black car with white doors cruised by slowly. There was a red bubble on its roof, and behind the wheel Sergeant Gumbrell was looking in our direction.

"The gum machine?" I asked.

"The police car," said Jenny. "We call it that because the light on top looks like a bubble-gum dispenser."

"What are you starin' at, Gumbrell?" shouted Fraser. "You got your mouth open like a jack fish in a school of minnows!"

Storm clouds swept across Sergeant Gumbrell's face; the gum machine continued down the street.

"Why don't you like Sergeant Gumbrell?" questioned Jenny.

Fraser growled as he proceeded into the smoke filled room called *Gentlemen Only*. "Hah! See you later."

As Jenny and I walked home, past the Hudson's Bay and Neely's Drug Store, Jenny asked, "You know that book Fraser gave me yesterday? I forgot it in his garage. You don't think he'd mind if we went in and got it, do you?"

"I guess not," I said.

When we got to the Blossom sisters' yard, there was a table on the lawn next to the fountain. It was laid with white linen and set with cups, saucers, plates and silver. Around it, there were six chairs.

I looked about. "Where is everybody?"

Jenny stood beneath the sign that read *Steel True – Blade Straight*. She put her hand on the door and looked back.

I looked to the alley, then to the porch. There was no one around. But as I followed Jenny into the garage, I glanced up. Smoky the crow stared down through billows of smoke.

"Edward, look!"

In the dark garage, a yellow light floated in the middle of the floor. The back of my neck turned cold. "What is it?"

The eerie light twisted and turned within itself, and through its glow I saw the face of the laughing dog.

"Stairs," pointed Jenny.

In the darkness, Fraser's oval carpet was rolled back, and a trap door was open in the floor. I put my hands into my pockets to stop them from shaking. Red carpeted steps led down into the glowing light.

Jenny was on her knees. "Edward. There's a room down there."

She stood, then placed one foot onto the first step. She took another step, and another, until only her head was showing above the floor. "Are you coming?"

"I guess so," I said. My mouth was dry.

At the bottom of the steps, we found ourselves in a small room decorated with gold wallpaper.

"What is this place?" said Jenny.

In front of us, there were three doors at different angles. The door to the left was draped in a dusty grey canvas, but the door in the middle and the one on the right were made of polished wood, each with a big brass doorknob. From somewhere close I heard the sound of a ticking clock. My heart pounded beneath my T-shirt.

"Maybe we better get back," I said.

Jenny twisted the knob on the middle door, and it clicked. She pushed, and we were in the warm glow of a fire-lit room. "Beautiful!"

"Should we go back now?"

The floor was covered with thick carpet in a Chinese pattern. A fire of logs burned on a wide hearth. A velvet chair and a small sofa faced each other in front of the fireplace; a purple dressing gown was thrown across the chair. There was a wooden desk and a case full of books, and against one wall, a table covered with bottles and test tubes, like a scientific experiment.

"A big chemistry set," said Jenny, "and a microscope."

Above the fireplace, there was a large mirror in a thick wooden frame and in front, on the mantel, a clutter of different things: a rack of smoking pipes, a magnifying glass, and some postcards stuck in place with a jackknife. There were also an embroidered slipper, a stuffed snake with stripes, a big harpoon, and a real revolver. Next to the fireplace hung a picture of a fat lady wearing a crown.

"Queen Victoria," said Jenny. "And look! Real bullet holes."

Below the picture, we saw holes in the wall spelling out the letters *V. R.*

"Sherlock Holmes did that – to honour his queen."

"Sherlock Holmes?"

"This is the sitting room of 221B Baker Street. Where the Great Detective lives – where he solves all his mysteries!"

From behind us came a loud *bong*. I jumped. A huge grandfather clock was next to the door.

"Maybe we better go back."

"But, what about the other rooms?"

We were now standing in front of the dusty grey canvas. With a great flourish, Jenny threw it aside. There was nothing but darkness.

"The light switch, Edward. Turn on the light!"

I flipped the switch next to the door, and as if a magician had waved his wand, we were staring down a long gaping tunnel. Twisted roots hung from the ceiling and walls. Bright light bulbs drooped away from us on a long looping wire.

"A secret passage."

"Should we go back?"

My knees trembled as we walked along the tunnel. The air was cold and the ground hard. Above us, heavy timbers were held in place by iron spikes.

"It goes under the alley," said Jenny. "The alley is right above us. And look!"

At the other end of the tunnel, a huge grey stone hung from the ceiling. Below it, there was a wheelbarrow and a shovel.

"It's Mountaintop Rock. We usually sit on top. But now," Jenny was staring at the underside of the big stone, "now we're standing below it." Then something caught her eye. She peered more closely. "See there, Edward, where the rock disappears into the dirt. It's…. Hand me the shovel." She took the shovel and rammed up hard. The shovel clanged, and bits of sand and gravel fell. She thrust once more, and we heard a dull hollow thud.

"Boost me."

I laced my fingers and Jenny placed one foot into my hands. I lifted her up, and she reached and pulled hard. Sand and gravel came down in my face, and we fell in a heap on the floor. In her hand was a flat metal box.

"An old paint set." Jenny wiped rust from the paint box with her T-shirt, and then pried open the lid. Inside were some twice-folded pieces of paper, which Jenny carefully removed. Underneath, all the little trays of paint were dry and cracked. The pages were very old.

"It's a typed letter."

"What does it say?"

"It says *'Dear Daisy.'*"

"Daisy?"

Jenny started reading:

From the Residence of the Superintendent
Jasper Park, Alberta, Canada
June 21, 1914
Dear Daisy:

I sit quietly this evening, taking in the fresh mountain air. This morning, however, I awoke to the sound of a shotgun blast fired by Rogers. He was chasing a pussy cat away from the chicken coop. Lady D and I laughed as we made ourselves ready here in these fine rooms we have been given in this lovely stone building.

"Stone building," exclaimed Jenny. "This letter was written at the Boulders."

She kept reading as we made our way back along the tunnel:

Our friend, Colonel S. Maynard Rogers, has lost little of the spunk he showed when he served with us in South Africa. It seems, however, he has far greater responsibilities now that he's the superintendent of Jasper Park – the cat and chickens are fine.

We've had a marvellous stay in these beautiful mountains. Your descriptions, Daisy, were perfect! While here, I have designed a golf course, laid the corner stone of a church, and tomorrow, I will have a good British go at whacking a pitch at a baseball game. All these endeavours to promote the Grand Trunk Pacific Railway, and to keep the Union Jack flying high above this alpine grandeur.

Jenny looked up from the letter. "Sir Arthur Conan Doyle did all those things in Jasper, in 1914. I bet he wrote this letter."

She kept reading:

The Musketeers are well. They see us off tomorrow at the train station. Before our departure, we're to have a final excursion – to the hill known as Old Fort Point. The view, they say, is breathtaking. While there we're promised some sport, which involves, I'm told, looking into the sky. Musketeer W still makes me laugh. Such a talent is Musketeer W.

Jenny looked up again, with a puzzled expression. "Musketeer W? The Musketeers?"

The highlight of our visit to Jasper was a journey by packhorse to Whirlpool River, or to be more exact, to the compliance of the Whirlpool and its sister river, the Athabasca. Our route followed the west bank of the Athabasca, along the Athabasca Trail.

We were placed in the capable hands of a packer, par excellence – a gentleman by the name of Closson Otto. He is typical of these fine mountain people – kind, understanding, and sensitive to the feelings of others. They are hearty folk, with a great desire to venture and endure.

This morning, as we rode the winding woody vale, Otto threw down before me a glove of challenge. "You are the creator of the world's greatest detective!" he said. "Can you tell us the location of Henry House?"

I know nothing of this house, I said. And so Otto told me the story of David Thompson, the great Welsh surveyor who discovered the Athabasca Pass, which as you know, Daisy, was the old route of the fur trade – up the Whirlpool River and eventually to the Pacific Ocean.

Jenny and I were now back in the room with the gold wallpaper. She continued reading the letter.

Thompson discovered the Athabasca Pass during the winter of 1811. While facing the hardships of a mountain crossing, he left a man named William Henry to build a supply depot, or fort, near what is now the town of Jasper. There is today a great mystery with respect to the exact location of Henry's original structure. It was built, it seems, on the shore of the Athabasca River near a rocky hill or promontory.

'I cannot make bricks without straw,' I told Otto, 'so give me, if you will, the details of the situation, and I will gather the straws we need.' I accepted Otto's challenge, and told him that before the day was out I would solve the great mystery of Henry House.

So, as our pack train trekked past foaming rapids into virgin upland, as the pleasant morning drifted by, I came to think that the mystery of this fur depot was a worthwhile project. For these are not fairy tales! We deal here with history, with the very lifeblood of this young country called Canada.

When the sun was high above the snow-capped peaks, we reached the

mouth of the Whirlpool. Closson Otto called a halt, and in a meadow car-
peted with mountain flowers, he spread a cloth and laid upon it a lunch
that would have brought envy to Simpson's-in-the-Strand. I reclined on one
elbow, and with a quiet smile of satisfaction said, "My deductive powers
have shown me the location of Henry House."

"Where?" Otto asked. "Tell me where."

"You must wait," said I. "All things are revealed in their natural
course."

"But how did you make this discovery," asked my guide.

"When you have eliminated all that is impossible, then what remains,
however improbable, must be the truth."

"There are only two more pages!" said Jenny. "Sir Arthur Conan
Doyle is going to reveal the location of Henry House!" She returned to
the letter.

As our mountain ponies carried us back along the Athabasca River, I
felt there was a story in me about David Thompson and William Henry,
and as I settled back in the saddle, as the pine needles crunched beneath my
pony's hooves, a new adventure took shape.

And so this evening, here in this house that Rogers has built of moun-
tain stone, with the stars out my window twinkling in a blue and luminous
sky, I shall bring my hawk-nosed detective and his bumbling doctor friend
to the beautiful mountains of Jasper.

Jenny looked astounded. "It's a Sherlock Holmes story."

I felt a shiver as I looked back along the tunnel.

"Edward, listen!" Jenny read.

THE MYSTERY OF HENRY HOUSE

By John H. Watson, M.D.

That my friend Sherlock Holmes and I had travelled for such a great dis-
tance to meet such an enemy, and that that enemy's proximity had been so
close for so long, spoke volumes: the man's abilities were equalled only by his
potential for evil.

Jenny gasped.

A journey by rail across the wide Dominion of Canada had brought Holmes and myself to beautiful Jasper Park, high in the Canadian Rockies. I had never seen Holmes so happy.

"Hah!" said he, joyously striking his alpenstock against the small wash of sandy beach he stood upon. "Watson! My dear fellow! Tell me! What Londoner would believe that a two-shilling ticket from Victoria Station could lead to such wild beauty as this? These mountains! This air!" Holmes raised his arms and took a deep breath. "Like the wet scent of a Surrey spring – mixed with the Christmas taste of a baked caramel apple." He gazed up from green water to a bare knoll, which lifted itself in two plateaus above us.

"We have sat idle too long, my friend! Too long in our damp Baker Street rooms, amid swirling fog, and the dreary clip-clop of hooves on cobble. Here!" shouted Holmes. "Here among these peaks of melting snow, do we draw our ease. Here at this spot where this small stream meets this mighty river, here we could pull our easy chairs up to the very hearthstone of our hearts. Watson! Here I would choose to live, or to die."

From behind us there came a reedy voice. "I could promise you one," it said, "but not the other." We turned, and not ten yards off among the pines stood a very tall, thin man. His brow sloped back in a white arch; his face was serpent-like, swaying from side to side. As he approached, his deep set, puckered eyes were blinking and he looked at Holmes in a strange peering sort of way.

Sensing danger, my hand reached into my Hudson's Bay coat for the comfort of my old army service revolver.

"Tut! Tut! Mr. Holmes," said the man. "You would trade your great wealth and consideration for this?"

"Professor Moriarty!" gasped Jenny. She held up the last page. "But, there's no more! We still don't know."

Above us, through the trap door, I heard my mom's voice.

"We better go," I said.

"But, Edward, we don't know what's behind the third door – the one on the right."

I started up the steps, and Jenny followed.

"And the smoke! Where does the smoke go?"

"What smoke?"

"The smoke from the fireplace in 221B."

We were back in the garage, standing in the yellow light.

"It must come up here," Jenny whispered, "into the old wood stove and out through the chimney, where Smoky sits."

We stepped from the garage into the bright sunshine. My mom, Mrs. Trotwood and Pat Blossom were sitting around the table.

"Edward! *What* have you been doing? You're filthy!"

"Jennifer? Was Mr. McKillop in there with you?" Mrs. Trotwood placed her teacup into its saucer and sniffed.

"No, I, we...." Jenny pulled the now crumpled post office letters from her pocket. "We got the mail." She put the letters on the table, but still had the pages from Sir Arthur Conan Doyle in her hand.

Mrs. Trotwood was staring at her letters, and my mom was still giving me her look. Pat Blossom peered at the pages in Jenny's hand, but said nothing as Jenny quickly put them back into her pocket.

My mom's voice was stern. "Edward, were you in Mr. McKillop's garage without his permission?"

Smoky the crow squawked from the roof of the garage.

"We...."

Jenny jumped in. "I thought I left my book in there. Mr. McKillop said pop in anytime."

"Did *we* get any mail, Edward?" asked my mom.

I reached into my pocket. "The letter from...." It was gone. Mom looked at me hopefully. I had to stare at my shoes. "Aunt Edie's letter...it didn't come."

"Oh," said Mom.

Just then, Fraser appeared at the gate. "Ladies! Nice to see your smiling faces." At the same time, Kate Blossom was coming down the steps with a tray of sandwiches and a big white cake.

"Jenny! Edward! Fraser! Come and have some lunch and a nice cup of tea."

Under her breath Mrs. Trotwood said, "It smells like Mr.

McKillop's already *had* his lunch."

"Ah! Kate," said Fraser. "All these years, I've never heard you say 'cup of tea,' without putting the word *nice* in front of it. A sandwich and a nice cup of tea. Wonderful!" He sat down next to Pat.

"Pat," Fraser went on. "I've read the 'The Adventure of the Blue Carbuncle,' again, and that goose is still a bird of great value." He laughed and took a sandwich. "It is one of your favourites, I know."

"Fraser, Pat is not reading as much as she used to," said Kate.

But Pat spoke up. "Sherlock Holmes reasoned that the man went upstairs with his hat in one hand and a lit candle in the other. I've always wondered why he would take his hat upstairs at all. Why wouldn't he leave it on the sideboard in the hallway?" She smiled. "And why would he put it anywhere but on his head?"

"True, Pat. True." said Fraser, taking a bite of sandwich. "But the Great Detective figured it all out." Fraser looked at me. "You'll have to read 'The Blue Carbuncle.' It's a wonderful Christmas story."

Pat sat up straight. "Sherlock Holmes 'was the best and wisest man it has ever been my great good fortune to know.' That's what Doctor Watson said."

"Ah, Pat, you're in fine form," said Fraser, taking another sandwich. "You're quotin' well."

Pat now looked quizzically at her sister. "Did I put sugar in my tea, Kate?"

"You did, Pat."

Fraser was chewing on his second sandwich. "Kate, let's head out tomorrow. You and Pat can paint while I fish."

"The doctor says Pat must take things a little easier now, Fraser. We're both having to slow down a little. But perhaps the children would like to go." Kate looked to my mom and Mrs. Trotwood.

"Well, Edward *has* been keeping his room very neat and tidy, lately," said Mom.

I thought again about the spiders.

"Mom, can we go fishing with Fraser?" Jenny asked. "Can we, please?"

Mrs. Trotwood glanced quickly at Fraser, then at Kate. "I don't think that's a very good idea."

"Please?"

"I don't...."

"Oh, they'll have a wonderful time, Honoria." Kate smiled, as she poured Mrs. Trotwood another cup of tea. "Fraser will look after them, and everything will be fine."

"You'd have to be up at the crack of dawn," Fraser said. "You'd have to be up with the birds."

"We'll be up with the birds," I said.

"And we'll catch a big fish!" said Jenny.

"Hah!" said Fraser taking another sandwich. "I always catch big fish."

Mrs. Trotwood sniffed, then took a sip of tea. "Well, maybe...."

CHAPTER 10

FISHING AT SIXTEEN-AND-A-HALF

When we arrived at Fraser's garage the next morning, the sun had not yet lifted from behind the Maligne Range. The sky was a swirl of gold and grey, and the birds were chirping for sunshine to warm the valley.

As we approached the door, Kate Blossom's voice came from inside: "So, probably tomorrow, Fraser, or maybe the next day, or...oh! The children."

Kate and Fraser were at the wooden table – he, drinking coffee from an old china mug; she, holding a red thermos bottle. The purple dressing gown was neatly folded on Fraser's bed.

"Here's some tea for you," said Kate, "and there's lots of things for making sandwiches." Jenny and I held high the brown bags of sandwiches our moms had made.

"Sandwiches? You don't need sandwiches when you fish with me. Butter and a frying pan. That's all you need. Let's go!" Fraser headed out the door.

Jenny and I could hardly contain our excitement. If the fish we were going to catch were as big as the smiles on our faces, it was going to be a wonderful day.

Fraser thumped his fist on the fender of Blue Lightning, and yellow dust flew in the air. "Best darn truck this side'a Hamilton, and they don't know how to make them any further east than that. OK, toss it in. The rods. The reels. All your implements of wilderness tackle. Blue Lightning's carried bigger loads than this." He was laughing as we got into the massive cab. The motor roared, and as we headed out of town, the valley filled with sunshine.

"Where are we going?" asked Jenny.

"Sixteen-and-a-Half."

"Sixteen-and-a-half, what?"

"Sixteen-and-a-Half Lake." Fraser shifted gears with one hand, and put snoose in his mouth with the other. He was steering with his elbow.

"Why is it called that?"

"In 1914, the superintendent of Jasper Park was a man by the name of Rogers, Colonel Rogers, a close friend of Sir Arthur Conan Doyle's. They were in the Boer War together. Rogers wanted to have a secret fishing place. So when the government was naming all the lakes, he made sure they left one with no name. It was 16-and-a-half miles out of town, so it's been called Sixteen-and-a-Half ever since."

So, sixteen-and-a-half miles down the south highway, Blue Lightning pulled over and we got out. There, perched on the back of the canvas canopy was Smoky the crow.

"Smoky, ya buzzard! You're up early." Fraser shook his head at the bird. "OK, get the stuff out, and don't leave nothin' in the cab. I'm not gonna lock'er up."

"Why?" asked Jenny.

"Because," said Fraser.

"Because why?"

"Because, don't ask so many questions. Now, get the stuff out."

"Why aren't we locking the doors?"

Fraser spit black stuff on the ground. "Because sometimes ya gotta come back faster than ya went."

"You mean we might be chased by a bear?"

"I mean a bear or a moose or an elk or maybe the Ghost of Christmas Past. Whatever! We won't be lockin' it up. And I've got the key."

There's a thrill in walking through the woods to a mountain lake. Straining your eyes ahead, the background of forest becomes a mirage and you think you see the water, but you don't. When you finally do, you look twice before you're certain the lake is really there.

"Isn't it beautiful," said Fraser, when the trees finally turned to water. "*This pale green-tinted light, as in forest aisles!*" he quoted.

The lake was still. Morning vapours hovered above it. Tall pines crowded down from the mountains to stand close against the shore, and somewhere on the far side, a lonely loon called out in the mist. About 20 feet out in the water, a widening circle appeared, as if someone had thrown a stone. "They're jumpin'," whispered Fraser. A soft wind lifted, and light sparkled on the lake. Millions of glinting ripples appeared before our eyes. Fraser lifted a clump of dead willow to reveal a small varnished rowboat. "Remember, no standing up in the boat. It's dangerous."

Now Fraser reached into his fishing bag and pulled out two long jangly contraptions made of wire, red beads, and thin pieces of shiny metal. At the end of each mechanism was a thin nylon leader that held a small sharp hook.

"Like giants' jewellery," said Jenny.

"Trolling lures," said Fraser. "This one's called a Ford Fender and these are Willow Leaves. Here's how you tie them on."

When the lures were tied, Fraser placed a hand on my shoulder. "Wiggins, I believe you'd make a good captain – you're courageous, strong, and courteous. Do you think you could handle the job?"

I felt my chest heave, and I straightened my shoulders.

"I'll do my best," I said.

"But can you row a boat? Cause that's the job of the captain."

I nodded eagerly.

"You *can*? Wonderful. Hoist anchor then, sir. And remember. No standing up."

We were off. Jenny sat in the front of the boat, and I was in the middle. Fraser took the big seat at the back.

"I'll be in charge of the food, the beer, and the Coca-Colas," said Fraser. "OK, Captain. Head for the other side."

I pulled on the oars, and the little boat drifted through the mist. When I lifted the oars, drops of water gently fell, breaking the reflection of the mountains and the sky. We were floating somewhere between the billowy clouds and the green sparkling water.

"Let's get these lines out," Fraser said. He reached under his seat and took out an old coffee can that spilled over with green moss. Carefully, he lifted a wriggling worm from beneath the moss and pushed it onto the sharp point of a hook. With strong fingers, he delicately skewered more worms over the barb and up the shank. Worm

after worm was skewered, until he had made a round wriggling ball. "You've got to dress it up like a Christmas tree," he said, dangling the slimy creation close to my nose. "It's got to look so good you'd eat it yourself." Then he held the ball of worms up to his own gaping mouth and looked at me sideways, like a ravenous worm-eating monster. He laughed, and I grimaced.

"I think I'd like to use the Silver Doctor instead of worms," said Jenny.

When we lowered the lines into the water, I pulled again on the oars, and the blades of the lures started to spin. They drifted away, sinking slowly and steadily, to do their work at the bottom of the lake.

"OK, now, Captain. Row steady and keep 'er straight." Fraser sat back and opened a bottle of beer. "Let's have a sandwich." He pulled bologna and a jar of Thousand Island sandwich spread from his tackle bag.

"Fraser?" asked Jenny. "What are we going to do with the fish when we catch it?" Fraser was spreading sandwich spread onto a piece of white bread.

"We're gonna whack its head over the gunwales until it's dead. OK, who likes the crust?" He held up a sandwich.

By mid-morning we had caught no fish. The sun was high, and the air was warm. Rods tipped, and our heads bobbed, and in my dream there was a tea party in a long sandy tunnel. My mom was dressed as an airmail letter, and Mrs. Trotwood was dressed as a sniffing bear. Between them sat Pat Blossom, wearing a baseball cap with a peak at the front and a peak at the back. From somewhere in the tea party of my mind I heard the sound of a splashing fountain. Kate Blossom was saying, "Nice cup of tea! Nice cup of tea!" But she was a black plastic cat, and her eyes looked back and forth continuously. The splashing grew louder and louder, and my neck felt sweaty and my head was hot, and, now, the splashing was everywhere and I opened my eyes to see Fraser standing up in the boat, with his back to me, peeing over the side.

From the other end of the boat came a yell. "Fraser! What are you doing?" Jenny stood up. "That's not nice!" The little boat lifted with a mighty jolt, and Fraser's arms flew into the air, and grabbed at nothing. Then the boat crashed down with a loud splash, and Fraser was gone.

"Hell's bells!" yelled Fraser, his arms thrashing wildly in the water. Sunshine made rainbows in the spray. "You little hoyden! You, you Moriarty!"

From across the lake a loon called out, and from above us in a tree, Smoky the crow cawed in a loud voice, "Hell's bells! Hell's bells!"

Jenny shouted, "I know who Moriarty is! He was the evil enemy of Sherlock Holmes. I'm not your friend if you think I'm a Moriarty!" she yelled.

There was another splash and a spray of water, and Fraser heaved a sopping leg into the boat. "I told you not to stand up!"

"You were standing up," said Jenny, "peeing over the side!"

"I had to!"

"You're not supposed to pee when you're in a boat!"

As the Captain, I felt at that point I should say something, but I didn't. Fraser rolled, drenched and dripping, into his seat, and again the little boat rocked up and down, in a cranky sort of way. On the floor, green and orange moss was smeared with Thousand Island sandwich spread, and my little craft now seemed in general disarray.

"Row back to shore!" ordered Fraser. Soon the gentle groaning of the oar locks was the only sound.

It was a long walk back up the path. I ate my sandwiches, and no one said a word. I thought about the tunnel under the alley, and worried about my mom's lost letter. When we got to Blue Lightning, Jenny turned quickly, bumping into me. "No!" she whispered. "This time I sit by the window."

I got in first, and Jenny jumped in beside me. She stared straight ahead.

Fraser was outside with his hands in his pockets. First he dug deep into his side pockets; then he tried the back ones. Then he reached into his shirt pocket, and then he looked down the path towards the lake. "Well. You can get out. We've lost the keys!"

We started the16-and-a-half miles back to Jasper on foot, Fraser in his wet clothes, Jenny saying nothing. Even when we crossed the bridge at Whirlpool River, where David Thompson had discovered the Athabasca Pass, Fraser was silent. The three of us just walked down the quiet road. When we got to the Valley of the Crooked Trees, we looked back along the highway and saw a big black car with dark windows approaching. It pulled up close and stopped.

Fraser looked at the licence plate.

The driver's window rolled down, and behind the wheel was a man with curly red hair. "Going to Jasper?" he said in a friendly way.

"That's where we're headed," said Fraser.

"Hop in."

Fraser opened the door and we looked inside. "Pretty fancy," he muttered.

In the back of the big car, we were separated from the driver by another dark window. The interior was panelled in shiny brown wood, and the seats were puffy and covered in soft leather.

The driver's voice came through a little speaker.

"'You folks live around here?"

"Know the area a bit," said Fraser.

"Looking for a couple of sisters that live in Jasper. Two old girls that do some painting?"

I started to speak, but Fraser kicked me on the ankle.

"Sorry, pal. Can't help you." Fraser snuggled his shoulders into the cushioned seat, and closed his eyes. Within a minute he was snoring.

When we got to Jasper, Fraser woke up and had the man with curly red hair drop us off at the end of our alley.

"Thanks for the lift," said Fraser.

"You're welcome," said the man with curly red hair. He stared straight into Jenny's eyes. "You have a face like an angel. Beautiful."

"Oh, thank you."

Fraser took Jenny by the arm, and gently drew her away.

As we walked up the alley, there were still no words. When we reached the garage, Fraser said, "Well, no fish, and a few mishaps. But, all in all, it wasn't a bad day, was it? I did entertain you a little."

Jenny looked up slowly.

"When you fall in the water," said Fraser, "you stir up a little muck. But it always settles. The next time, we'll catch a big fish. I promise." He gave Jenny a smile.

Jenny waited before she smiled back. But she did. "And will we use the Silver Doctor?"

"You bet we will." Fraser laughed. And now the water was clear, Jenny laughed, too.

"Why didn't we tell the man about Kate and Pat?" I asked.

"Why bother two sweet ladies with some fancy guy in a rented car?"

"Is he the special friend who's coming to visit?" asked Jenny.

"No, he's not."

"And what's a hoyden?"

Fraser thought for a moment. "A hoyden? A hoyden is a bold boisterous girl." He laughed again and headed for the yard. "Now, what did I do with those extra keys."

CHAPTER 11

THE ONE THAT GOT AWAY

I dropped all my trucks and cars into the Dinky toy sandpit. "My mom says we're staying at the Blossom sisters' tonight because our parents are going to the big dance at the Lodge. And we're supposed to take our pyjamas because the dance won't be over till late. And we're having supper there, too," I said excitedly.

"I know that," said Jenny. "And Fraser's having supper with us. Then we're going fishing. This time, he says, we're going to catch a *huge* fish. And I know something else." Jenny took her notebook from her pocket and flipped it open. "Pat Blossom might have to live in a home in Calgary because she can't remember things." Jenny looked around as if someone might be listening. "Do you think the man in the car has come to pick her up?"

"The man with curly red hair? Is he going to take her away?"

Above us, we heard a flapping of wings, and Smoky the crow flew into the sky. I followed his flight, but he passed in front of the sun and the brilliant glare hurt my eyes.

Jenny closed her notebook.

Later that afternoon, we were having our picture taken in the front yard. Mr. Trotwood's camera sat perched on its tripod. "Lovely!" he said, "You ladies look lovely." He placed one eye to the viewfinder "OK.... I've got Pyramid Mountain. Move over, Jenny. Closer, Edward. Closer. Tom, your tie is crooked."

"Oh, aye! No crooked ties at Jasper Park Lodge!"

"Ready, now. Wait. Wait till I get there." The timer whirred as Mr. Trotwood ran into the shot. "Say cheese!" And that happy moment was held forever – two families on a warm summer afternoon, the women smiling in flared dresses and beauty parlor hairdos; the men standing straight, in their jackets and bow ties. In front, two children – a girl and boy – are squirming.

Dinner at Kate and Pat's was at six o'clock. The kitchen door opened without warning. "Hello, this house!"

"Come in!" said Kate. "My goodness, Fraser. Don't you look nice. Your tweed suit, your white shirt and your red tartan tie."

"You're all dressed up," said Jenny.

Fraser put his hands in his pockets and pulled up his baggy pant legs. "Hah!"

"Your Argyle socks and your brown brogues," Kate commented. "What *is* the occasion?"

"We're goin' to the Lodge for banana splits!"

"The Lodge?" Jenny frowned. "I thought we were going fishing."

Dinner was a noisy affair, with the passing of dishes and the serving of food, and Fraser answering questions about why we weren't going fishing.

When she had finished her meal, Pat Blossom folded her hands in front of her. "I know the truck will be crowded," she said, "but, I think I should like to go to the new Jasper Park Lodge."

"Crowded?" said Fraser. "We'll be cozy. Packed in like seeds in a pine cone. Let's go!"

Blue Lightning headed down the south highway, and turned left at the sign that said Old Fort Point. Fraser was right. We were packed in like seeds in a pine cone: Jenny sat on Kate's lap, and I scrunched in front of Pat gripping the dashboard.

As we drove onto the iron bridge that crossed the Athabasca River, Kate said, "I'm sure we'll see your parents at the Lodge."

Fraser stepped on the gas. "Why bother them while they're havin' all that fun?"

On the other side of the bridge, the road swept down to the left into a forest of jack pine and black poplar. Jenny turned and looked back. "Up there," she said. "That's the top of Old Fort Point. From there, you can see the whole valley and all the mountains."

Pat stared through the windshield as the truck carried us through a long lane of tall trees. Her lips moved and her chin shook gently. "Like a sunlit banner," she said to no one in particular. "A sunlit banner...." She searched deep in her mind.

"On a storm sky," said Kate. "You remember, Pat, the first time we flew a kite from the top of Old Fort Point."

Pat's lips trembled. "We, we were with Sir Arthur."

"Sir Arthur Conan Doyle!" said Jenny. "You flew a kite with Sir Arthur Conan Doyle?"

The kite drifted from Pat's mind, "We…, what was I saying, Kate?"

"You remember, dear. Lady Doyle was with us, and Colonel and Mrs. Rogers. And we all helped to make the kite at the Boulders, in the Rogers' living room. Then we rode the ponies out to Old Fort Point, and crossed the wooden bridge, and hiked the trail to the top. We took turns holding the string, and the kite flew high across the valley. Sir Arthur said it was the most beautiful sight he had ever seen. Then the clouds rolled in from the west, and Sir Arthur said the kite was like a sunlit banner on a storm sky. That's what he said, Pat. Like a sunlit banner on a storm sky."

"I let it go," Pat said. "I let it go."

Kate's eyes were now moist with tears. She lifted her chin. "Sir Arthur was a kind man, like our daddy. They were the best of friends."

"Friends?" questioned Jenny. "They were friends?"

"The Doyles were our neighbours in Hindhead. Daddy and Sir Arthur served together in South Africa."

"We flew a kite," said Pat, "from the top of Old Fort Point."

"We did, Pat. June 22, 1914, seven days before the start of the First World War."

"Daddy died in the War," Pat murmured. She was staring again through the windshield. "I let it go. I let it go."

Now the only sound was the rumbling of the truck as we travelled along the road to the Lodge.

"He didn't really die *in* the war, Pat. He died before the war. Our daddy was a remarkable mediator. He was at the Foreign Office, at Whitehall. But he wasn't, he wasn't...."

"A spy?" I said.

"No, he wasn't – " Kate's thought ended.

Fraser tried to be cheerful. "Remember the last time we flew a kite from Old Fort Point?"

"I do," said Kate, smiling through her tears. "And I bet a nickel you do, too."

Fraser thumped the steering wheel. "When is our special friend arriving?" He said the words again sarcastically: "*special friend.* And why does it have to be such a big secret?"

"She'll be here soon," said Kate.

Jenny's ponytail flicked my face as she looked from Kate to Fraser. "Your special friend is a lady?"

Fraser geared down again, and we turned sharply to the right.

"Lac Beauvert," said Kate, clapping her hands. "The water is as lovely as ever!"

The road now gripped the edge of a brilliant green lake. Sunshine settled onto its surface, and its colour changed before our eyes – from green to blue, and back to green, like the feathers of a peacock. Across the lake, below the mountain shaped like a sleeping Indian, rolling

lawns and stone terraces reached down to touch the shore.

"The Lodge," said Fraser, "a mountain kingdom of varnished pine and glacial stone. The long building in the middle, Wiggins, that's where your dad's been working – full of ballrooms and restaurants and fancy lounges. The log cottages along the front, that's where all the tourists stay."

"Stop here, please," said Pat, suddenly.

Blue Lightning slowed to a crawl, and we pulled up next to a small bay nestled among the trees. We all got out.

"The 14th tee," said Kate. "Pat's special spot."

On the other side of the bay lay a hummock of land covered with grass. Sticking out of it was a thin pole with a triangular flag attached.

Kate reached out and took her sister's hand.

"There wasn't a golf course when we first came," said Pat, squinting her eyes towards the water's edge. The water was so clear that the bottom of the bay was as easy to see as the ground around it. The shoreline seemed to just drift away, deep into the centre of the lake. "My sister and I worked at the Lodge when it was Tent City."

Kate put her arm around Pat's shoulder.

"Tent City?" I asked.

"When the railway arrived," Pat hesitated. "Visitors came from all over the world. They were met, at, at…" she struggled.

"At the train station, Pat. Visitors were met at the train station by horse and carriage and brought to the Lodge to be wined and dined. In those days, the shoreline of Lac Beauvert was dotted with tents, lovely white canvas tents with wooden floors and walls. In the evening, guests would visit with each other or read or play cards. The ladies would dress in lovely gowns and big hats, and the men looked smart in their evening clothes."

"What was your job at Tent City?" asked Jenny.

Kate looked into Pat's eyes as Jenny asked the question. "We were char girls," said Pat. But her thoughts were lost again somewhere beneath the green water.

"Char girls made the beds," said Kate. "They served the food, lit the fires, and kept things tidy. Char girls did all the chores, didn't they, Pat? And you got to live all summer in a tent by the lake."

"Was it fun living in a tent?" Jenny asked Kate.

"I didn't work at Tent City, Jenny."

"But, Pat said, her sister."

"I was not that sister."

"Winnifred," said Pat. "Winnifred and I worked at Tent City."

"You have another sister?"

Kate smiled and started to speak, but a loud caw broke the stillness. With a rapid flapping of wings, Smoky the crow lifted himself from the fender of the truck and flew out, low across the bay. His wing tips touched and made gentle ripples.

"He's taking a short cut," yelled Fraser. "Let's beat him and get to those banana splits!"

Blue Lightning took off following the crooked arm of the lake, past the golf course, and through an avenue of big trees until we came to a street lined with little log cottages and old fashioned lamp posts. Between the cottages and the lake, there were flagstone patios and rolling lawns. Everywhere we looked, we saw beautiful flower beds bursting with colour.

When we arrived at the canopy-covered entrance, the lobby was busy. Open-air limousines drove up, stopped and dropped off tourists, while bellhops in green uniforms, their arms full of luggage, told people to "have a wonderful stay."

From somewhere deep inside the main building, we heard a choir singing. "*Bali Ha'i may call you....*"

"The Jasper Glee Club," said Kate. "Oh, this is so exciting!"

Fraser parked Blue Lightning so close to the main door that the endless line of limos had to manoeuvre carefully around him.

"Are we allowed to park this close?" asked Jenny.

"You don't want to walk all the way from the parking lot, do you?" Fraser said. He took Pat by the arm and headed for the doors.

"Oh, excuse me, sir." A doorman wearing a pillbox hat stepped up smartly. "You're parked a little close."

"How goes the battle, young fella?" Fraser slipped something into the doorman's hand. "Put that towards your university education. We won't be long."

Without lowering his chin, the doorman looked down into his palm. "Oh, certainly, sir. That's fine, sir. Just leave the truck right there, sir." He gave Fraser a crisp salute. "The lobby is straight ahead, folks. Have a wonderful stay!"

Fraser took Pat's arm again, and we strolled into the Jasper Park Lodge.

"Oh, my goodness. It's beautiful," cried Kate.

The vast hall in which we stood was filled with rustic grandeur. Its ceiling lifted to a great height, supported in the middle by a massive stone fireplace. A fire blazed in the hearth below. From all around the room, mounted animal heads stared down – a deer, a bear, a moose, a mountain goat – and everywhere their glassy eyes looked, there were people – some writing, some reading, some playing cards. But the very best thing about the big room was the cowboy furniture. Tables and chairs were made of peeled and varnished logs; couches and divans carved from twisted roots and gnarled branches. And above it all, the room was aglow, lit by thousands of tiny lights twinkling from heavy iron chandeliers.

"Like in the movies," I commented aloud.

"Come on!" said Fraser. "Let's take a gander out the window."

The far wall of the room was a long row of windows that looked down onto Lac Beauvert. Beyond the line of jagged trees on the other side, a mountain taller than all the rest rose up to touch the sky. Covered in snow and capped in ice, its reverse image was mirrored perfectly on the calm water.

"Mount Edith Cavell," said Kate, "named for a brave nurse who died helping others. Its glacier is shaped like an angel."

As Kate spoke, a tint of early sunset caught the mountain's face, and again the waters of Lac Beauvert changed – from pale aquamarine to deep dusty pink. Now, all along the lake, the lawns and flower gardens were bathed in evening glow.

Fraser slipped his arm around Kate's shoulder. "Enough sad stories. Look at that guy down there. He could be in the circus."

Below us, on the path that went along the lake, a white uniformed waiter was riding a bicycle. He used one hand to steer and the other to balance a full tray of food perched on his shoulder.

"Hah! Think he delivers to town?" Fraser laughed. "Where's the snack bar? I wanna banana split."

The lobby was equally as spacious on the other side of the fireplace, where again, people relaxed in the beautiful furniture. As we walked along the wall of windows, I felt something tugging at my T-shirt. I stopped, and Jenny walked right into me.

"Keep going! Keep going!" she whispered.

"What?"

"Keep going! It's the man with curly red hair."

"What?"

"The man that's going to take Pat away. The man in the big car."

"Where?"

"By the fireplace. Don't look! Keep going!"

The singing voices of the glee club were now getting louder.

"Here's the dining room," said Fraser.

We looked into another big room full of people eating dinner. The round tables at which they sat were set with white cloths and fancy china, and in the centre of the room, among all the tables, water from a fountain was shooting straight up in the air. The sound of its splashing mingled with the chattering of people and the voices of the Jasper Glee Club, whose members were lined up on a stage at the other end. In the very middle of the singers, we could see Jenny's mom, her mouth a little wider, her voice a little louder than all the rest. In front, with his back towards us, Sergeant Gumbrell waved his arms about as he led the singing.

"I'm gonna wash that man right outa my hair. I'm gonna wash that man right outa my hair and send him on his way."

I turned and looked back at the fireplace. Sure enough, there was the man with curly red hair sitting alone at a table stacked with writing paper. He was reading intently.

"Edward, look! There's your mom and dad." Kate pointed, standing on her tiptoes. "And there's *your* dad, too, Jenny. And your mother – she's singing her heart out. Isn't it lovely?" Kate was waving. "Oh, they're enjoying the party."

"Let's not bother them," said Fraser. "Here's the snack bar. Banana splits," he said to the waitress. "Five of your very best!"

The snack bar was actually part of the dining room, but had been sectioned off by a large, sliding glass door.

It wasn't long before a man dressed in a black jacket and pants with stripes, hovered above our table. He was holding a long, narrow dish of ice cream with flags sticking out of it.

"Good evening," he said, tilting his head to one side. "I am Hildebrandt, the maître d'hotel." He bowed. "Your banana splits have arrived."

Hildebrandt had a French accent, and his mouth opened very little when he talked. He lowered the first banana split in front of Kate. "C'est pour vous, Madame."

"Oh. My goodness! Thank you."

Hildebrandt bowed again and stepped back a little. "An exquisite creation – fresh fruit, with three flavors of ice cream, chocolate sauce and a delicate Chantilly." He touched the tips of his fingers to his lips. "Garnished with crushed nuts and a maraschino cherry."

"And a lovely Royal Ensign," noted Kate.

With a precise movement, Hildebrandt took a small lighter from his waistcoat pocket. He flicked it once, and a tiny flame popped up. The flame touched thin grey sticks at either end of the ice cream.

"Sparklers!" exclaimed Jenny.

Kate gasped, her face aglow in a glitter of white light. "Oh, my," she whispered.

"Encore," Hildebrandt said, stepping aside majestically revealing two smiling waitresses, each holding two more banana splits. They stepped forward and the whole table shimmered.

"Good show!" said Fraser, slipping something into Hildebrandt's hand.

"Merci, monsieur." The maître d'hotel bowed lower than ever, and then, without seeming to open his mouth, said, "Have a wonderful stay."

"We will," said Fraser, "we will." And he used a long silver spoon to dig into his banana split.

"Delicious!" said Jenny. "Thank you, Fraser."

As we scooped up the last mouthfuls of ice cream, Fraser sat back in his chair and snapped his suspenders. "I'm just gonna pop out for a minute and see which way the wind's blowin'." He stood up and hitched his baggy pants. "I'll be back real quick," and he headed out of the snack bar.

Jenny hopped off her chair. "Shall we look through the glass door?"

"Certainly," said Kate.

Before Kate and Pat got to the glass door, I whispered to Jenny, "What if the man with curly red hair sees us when we leave? He'll want to take Pat to Calgary. Should we tell Fraser?"

"There he is," pointed Jenny.

"The man...?"

"No. Fraser. Look!"

The tables in the dining room had been pulled back to the walls, but the floor was now crowded with dancing people. The orchestra was on stage, and all around the pond, people were doing fancy footsteps. The water from the fountain gurgled high above their heads.

"Where's he going?" asked Jenny. Her nose was close to the glass.

Kate and Pat stood behind us now, as Fraser walked straight into the middle of the dance floor.

The music in the dining room grew louder, and pounding feet made everything shake. Sergeant Gumbrell was now on stage uncoiling a microphone, like he was getting ready to sing. Suddenly, Fraser came back out of the crowd.

"He's walking funny," said Jenny.

"Like an old sailor home from sea," said Kate.

Fraser headed quickly for the lobby. Pat's eyes narrowed as she stared. "Fraser..."

"He didn't!" said Kate.

"I think he did," said Pat.

Kate shook her head. "Surely, he didn't."

By the time we reached the entrance of the dining room, Fraser was halfway towards the big fireplace.

"Time to skedaddle," he yelled, and as he did, the man with the curly red hair looked up. Then a loud voice boomed over the loud speakers from the dining room.

"McKillop! You...you...," Sergeant Gumbrell sputtered. He dropped his microphone, leaped from the stage, and fought his way across the dance floor.

On the other side of the fireplace, Fraser now started running for the door. "Let's go!" he shouted.

The man with curly red hair stood up. "Excuse me. Could I talk with you for a moment, please?"

Kate and Jenny moved quickly. I grabbed Pat by the arm. Suddenly we were bolting for the door as fast as eight legs and a walking stick could carry us.

"McKillop! You!" Sergeant Gumbrell had struggled through the dancers and was now knocking over cowboy furniture in the lobby. "McKillop!" his voice boomed. But Fraser was outside, headed for the truck.

As we flew past the doorman, he saluted. "Hope you had a wonderful stay."

"We did!" yelled Fraser. "It was a lot of fun!"

We all piled into Blue Lightning. Fraser took off so fast the dust flew from under the canvas flaps, and a surprised waiter rode his bicycle into a tree. Sergeant Gumbrell stood beneath the canopy shaking his fist, and beside him Hildebrandt's usually closed mouth was open wide.

Fraser was laughing as we roared by all the little log cottages. He sat back gripping the steering wheel, his right leg looking uncomfortably straight. From his ankle to his thigh, his pant leg seemed to be twisting around like crazy. I looked down beneath the dashboard.

"Fraser…?" I started to question, but the answer to my question showed itself soon enough. There, sticking out of Fraser's pant leg, was the head of a huge fish. It stared up at me with one big eye, and I yelled, "A fish! A fish!"

Jenny screamed. "Fraser! Stop the truck! Stop! Stop!"

Fraser stepped on the gas. "You wanted a big fish. And I caught you one. A real big one!" He took off, driving the truck like a racecar.

"Fraser, what have you done?" cried Kate.

"Hah! I just moseyed over to that fancy fish pond and dangled my brogue over all those big beggars."

The fish had now flapped its way out of Fraser's pants and was beating its tail on the floor. Jenny was still screaming, trying to pick it up. "Stop the truck! Stop the truck!"

"You had a fishing line," said Kate. "A fishing line, down your trousers."

"The Silver Doctor," hooted Fraser. He coaxed Blue Lightning even faster. "My favourite fly, sticking out the cuff of my pants. And the big beggar chomped on it. I just hauled him right up my pant leg."

Pat was laughing as the big fish flapped all over the inside of the truck. Jenny was still screaming. "Stop the truck! Stop the truck!"

"Not till we get home!"

"Fraser!" Jenny yelled her very loudest. "You're an evil person! You're a Moriarty! I'm not your friend! Stop this truck!"

A long, high-pitched wailing came from behind. Fraser looked into the rear view mirror. "Gumbrell," he muttered, gripping the steering wheel even tighter. "In the gum machine." A reflection of red light flashed in the cab. Fraser straightened his arms and drove even faster.

By now the huge fish had landed onto Jenny's lap, and its big fat tail was slapping her comically in the face.

Kate's back straightened. "Fraser, stop the truck now. Please!" The words were hardly out of her mouth when Blue Lightning pulled up at the small bay by the 14th tee.

"Edward, the door," yelled Jenny. "Open the door!"

I pulled hard on the handle and threw myself out. Jenny was behind me, the enormous fish kicking in her arms. The gum machine was approaching fast, and behind it, the grey Chevy.

Jenny, with both arms wrapped around the fish, was running down to the bay. I followed, stumbling and tripping over rocks and bushes.

"Are you gonna throw it in?" I yelled.

"Yes." She was wading into the lake.

"It's beautiful. A giant rainbow trout."

The water was up to Jenny's thighs as she used both hands to lower the fish into the lake. She held it gently, coaxing it with her fingers. "You're all right, fish," she said. "You're all right." She moved her hands along its body, and its fins started to move. Then with a slow kick of its tail, it wiggled itself out of her hands and dropped below the surface. It stopped, quivered slightly, then swam into the darkness.

Jenny and I turned in the water to see the police car and the grey

Chevy, now at the scene of the crime.

"A fish down my pants?" Fraser yelled. "Gumbrell, give your head a shake! How could I get a fish down my pants?"

"McKillop, you had a rainbow trout in your trousers. That's a crime."

Our parents were standing outside the Chevy. My mom and dad and Mr. Trotwood were trying not to smile. Mrs. Trotwood looked very serious.

"Don't try to outsmart me, McKillop!" Sergeant Gumbrell and Fraser were nose to nose. "*You* had a fish in your pants."

"No, I didn't."

"Yes, you did."

"No! I did not!"

And so the grim struggle continued, and now Mrs. Trotwood, too, was smiling, as she held fast to her husband's arm.

The two adversaries were still locked in fiery battle as golden sunset started to pour through the cracks in the trees and glitter down onto the small bay by the 14th tee.

"Evening comes," said Dad happily, "and robes the mountains, and buttons them up with stars." And as he said that, the moon poked its shining head above Tekarra Mountain and our moms and dads hugged us good night. As we climbed back into Blue Lightning, we listened and heard from far across the lake, the music from the shores of Lac Beauvert.

CHAPTER 12

A CASE OF IDENTITY

"Well, you wanted a big fish, and you got it. Now nobody's talkin' to me." Fraser folded his tea towel and hung it on the handle of the oven door.

We were back at the Blossom sisters' Donald Duck House. Jenny and I were in our pyjamas helping Fraser and Kate with the dishes. Pat was sitting at the kitchen table.

Fraser headed for the door, but a noise from outside stopped him.

"Kate," said Pat. "It's – "

Before she could finish, the door of the porch slammed, and we heard a knock.

Pat stood up. "Jean! Jean has arrived!"

The kitchen door opened, and there in the darkness stood a lady with long brown hair. She was holding two small suitcases. "Aunt Kate!" she cried.

"Jean. It *is* you." Kate opened her arms, and the lady rushed in.

"Hi, Aunt Pat." The lady smiled over Kate's shoulder. "How are you?"

"Jean. Oh, Jean."

And now the three women were hugging in the middle of the kitchen.

"I came by train."

"But, we could have met you," Kate said.

The lady was still smiling. "No one bothered me. I walked down the alley." She laughed as she looked above the sink. "The cat I gave you is still ticking."

"It's lunchtime," said Pat.

"What's that, Aunt Pat?"

"It's lunchtime. The clock stopped, at lunchtime."

"I guess then, it is, Aunt Pat."

Pat's hands went back to the fold in her cardigan.

"Oh, we are going to have such a wonderful time," said Kate with delight. "Let me look at you, Jean. One whole year and now a married woman."

The lady laughed again, and tilting her head back, shook her hair. She turned to Fraser. "My hero!" She put her arms around his neck and kissed his cheek. "How are you?"

"I'm well, Jean. Congratulations on your marriage."

"Aw, he's just some Joe."

"He's a lucky guy. I'm sure you're happy."

Sadness briefly shadowed the lady's face but, just as quickly, she smiled and said, "I'm happy to be here."

Fraser stepped away from the door. "How long?"

"A week, maybe. Then I'm off." She turned to Jenny and me. "I haven't met you guys." She offered her hand to Jenny. "You look like someone I used to know."

"Meet Jenny and Edward," said Kate. "They're staying with us tonight while their parents are dancing at the Lodge."

"At the Lodge!" The lady was laughing again. "I almost stayed there once."

Kate continued the introduction. "You didn't meet Jenny last summer, and Edward has just arrived from England. Children, this is our special friend, Jean."

"I'm off, then," said Fraser. "I'll see you all tomorrow."

"But, Fraser, I just got here." Jean took him by the arm. "He's leaving us for Sherlock Holmes, isn't he, Aunt Pat?"

Pat was sitting again at the kitchen table. "Sherlock Holmes?"

"Of course, Aunt Pat."

"You remember, Pat," said Kate. "Sherlock Holmes. This afternoon. We talked about Sir Arthur." She spoke softly to Jean. "Sometimes everything is fine, and then…" Kate raised her arms at a loss.

"Everything's gonna be all right," said Fraser. "I'll see you all tomorrow."

"For sure, Fraser," said Jean. "And while I'm here we'll build a kite."

"Yes. A kite," said Pat. "We'll build a kite."

Fraser stepped into the porch. "We will for sure, Pat."

Pat's eyes brightened. "Fraser – "

"Yeah, Pat?"

"That was a lovely fish you caught tonight. It was a real beauty."

"Thanks, Pat."

That night, Jenny and I slept in Donald Duck's eyes.

"You're in the bedroom upstairs on the left, Jenny," said Kate, "and Edward, you take the one on the right. Jean, you look so tired, my dear. You'll be staying down here, in the back bedroom."

"Oh, thanks, Aunt Kate, but can't we stay up for a while and talk?"

"We can. But first, it's B-E-D for all children." Kate smiled. "Mother used to say that, didn't she, Pat?"

The three women escorted Jenny and me up the stairs and tucked us in with good night and God bless. When the lights were out and their chattering voices were a far off hum from the kitchen below, Jenny rapped a familiar but incomplete communiqué on the wall between us.

Tap! Tap! Tap-tap! Tap! and I answered, *Tap! Tap!*

And as I fell asleep, I dreamt of the giant rainbow trout moving like a slow torpedo at the bottom of Lac Beauvert, and in my dream I swam with the big fish until it saw me, and then it turned, and with its mouth wide open it came in my direction, whispering: "Edward, Edward."

"Wake up! Wake up!"

"Whaa?"

"There's a noise. Outside."

I opened my eyes to see Jenny beside the bed in her pyjamas.

"People are talking," she said in a whisper, "down in the yard."

Behind her the moon was bright and full through the open window.

"Talking?" I stammered.

"And everyone's gone to bed."

I jumped up.

"Listen!" We crouched beneath the window in a fall of soft moonlight.

Through the splashing of the fountain, we heard a woman's voice: "It's comforting," the woman said, "the air in Jasper is so comforting."

"That's Jean," said Jenny. Her eyes were wide open.

Below us in the darkness, Jean took a deep breath. "It's like when I was a little girl, my mother would pour lavender water into the rinse for her hair, and she smelled so beautiful. And then we would go to the movies on Wilshire and sit in the shadows of the silver screen and watch Katherine Hepburn or Jean Talmadge, or Jean Harlow, and I would snuggle up to my mother and smell the popcorn and the lavender, and that's what the air in Jasper smells like to me, my mother – full of love and comfort."

Then a man's voice said, "Why is everybody always tryin' to figure out what the air in Jasper smells like? It smells like trees."

Jenny grabbed my arm and whispered loudly, "Fraser!"

"It's a lot different from Arbol Drive," said Jean.

"Everything's different from Arbol Drive," said Fraser.

Then we heard only the sound of the splashing fountain.

"I'm sorry I couldn't send you an invitation," Jean said eventually. "It all happened, so quickly."

"Aw, well. I was probably pretty busy. There was about as much chance of me showing up at your wedding," he paused, "as there was of Tippy being there. That would have been great – me and Tippy at your wedding."

"Poor Tippy," said Jean. "He could have been as noisy as he liked. But it would have been nice to have had one friend there."

Slowly, Jenny and I lifted our heads above the sill of the window. In the yard moonlight glittered on the fountain.

"You'll never love anybody like you loved Tippy," said Fraser.

"Everybody I ever loved, I still love a little."

"Yeah, but not enough."

"Maybe not enough, right now."

"That's what you said last summer."

Again, Jean breathed in the cool night air. "Look at all the stars, Fraser. Millions and millions of stars."

And now Jenny and I could see them, Jean and Fraser, two shadowy shapes, sitting together on the bench by the book barrel.

"The marriage. It's not so good?" asked Fraser.

"It's not easy, up there in the stars."

From the blackness that was the roof of the garage came a cranky caw, and a glint of light flashed from a shiny beak. Claws scratched on the shingles, and Smoky the crow hopped up and down.

"He's ready to go," said Fraser. "Would you like to come?"

"Not tonight, Fraser. Thanks anyway."

Suddenly there was a loud hollow clang from the other side of the hedge, and Jean jumped up. "Besides, I'm still afraid of being eaten by bears."

Fraser reached out and took her hand, and she sat back down. "We're not on their menu," he said. "Bears don't go around eating human beings because they're hungry.

"Well, it's still pretty scary for a big city girl."

"Any wild animals deserve respect. If you spook a bear, you could

get into trouble, or worse, if you get between a mother and a cub, you can count on flying claws and sharp teeth." Fraser put his arm around Jean. "A mother bear always looks after her young."

"Maybe I wish I'd been born a bear."

"Ah, but bears don't use cream rinse."

Jean laughed, tilting her head back; her hair seemed white in the moonlight.

"Fraser, what I *would* like is something to read. I haven't read the Great Detective for ages."

Fraser reached into the book barrel. "Here's *The Adventures of Sherlock Holmes.* Try the third story, 'A Case of Identity.' About a beautiful woman searching for her lost lover."

"Does she find him?"

"You'll have to read it," he said.

They both laughed and Jean snuggled up to him.

"In the first sentence of that story," said Fraser, "Sherlock tells Dr. Watson that *'life is infinitely stranger than anything man could ever invent.'*"

"True," said Jean. "Who would believe that two crazy people like you and me could be searching so much for themselves – one up there in the stars – and the other...." They both laughed again, and somehow now the magic of the moonlight made her hair flash like gold.

"Good night, Jean."

"Good night, my hero."

Below us, the porch door opened and closed, and Jean came into the house. Fraser looked up at Smoky on the roof and then walked out into the alley.

"Where's he going?" said Jenny.

"Maybe he's searching for something."

"Maybe Tippy."

"Or Winnifred."

In the darkness on the other side of the garage, Blue Lightning rumbled to life. The hum of the motor hung in the air and then drifted down the alley. The moon was huge in the sky, and Jenny and I were now alone. We sat beneath the window in the moonlight and listened to the splashing fountain.

"I guess it's time to go to bed," said Jenny.

Before I fell asleep again that night, I rapped on the wall. *Tap! Tap! Tap-tap! Tap!* And Jenny answered, *Tap! Tap!*

CHAPTER 13

CLIMBING THE CASTLE TOWER

After breakfast, the next morning, I had news for Jenny. "My dad's going to fix the bell in the castle tower. And if we behave ourselves, *we* can go with him."

"The castle tower at the church?" Jenny unwrapped a third or fourth stick of gum and popped it into her mouth. "The castle tower is really high." She offered me a stick. "When is he going?"

"Before church starts. This morning. The minister can't ring the bell till my dad fixes the wooden thing that holds it up there. After that, you and I are going to attend the Sunday morning service with our parents."

"The very top of the castle tower?" Jenny was chewing hard on her gum.

"Are you afraid of heights?" I asked.

"Me? Afraid? No! I'm not afraid. Are you?"

"I'm not really sure. I've never been high up before."

"The castle tower," said Jenny, putting another stick of gum into her mouth, "is really high up."

One hour before the service started, Jenny and I walked with my dad up Larch Avenue and down to the cream-coloured church on Geikie Street. The three of us were dressed in our Sunday best, my dad carrying his tool box.

"Welcome!" said the minister, smiling from beneath an archway that led to big brown doors. "Welcome to the Church of St. Mary's and St. George. I'm Father Robinson." He was dressed in a long black robe that buttoned up the front, and around his neck hung a big silver cross. His eyes sparkled when he talked, and he seemed always to be smiling. His hair was cut in a flat-top brush cut.

"The soul," he said, looking up at the church with great pride, "the soul lifts up with the eyes, does it not?"

"My God, Father," said Dad, putting down his tool box, "and I say that with honest reverence. This is a beautiful building. It's like a young cathedral."

Father Robinson laughed. "A most whimsical thing to say." He winked at my dad. "A rock-solid little church. Simple, but full of dignity. It was built in 1927 – not a lot of history, but it's all our own."

"A magnificent kirk!" said Dad. "Stone buttresses and crenellation. Arched doorways and gothic windows. A true glory of gables. Such beauty! Such proportion."

"And all sitting on a hefty split-stone foundation," bragged Father Robinson as he placed one hand on my shoulder and the other on Jenny's. "Upon this rock I shall build my church! said our dear Lord."

"...with faith, hope, and love!" My dad picked up his tool box. "But the greatest of these...."

"...is love!" said Father Robinson. His face was radiant. "The Bible can teach us much about the mysteries of life. And thank God for the mystery. Without it, our lives wouldn't be very interesting." As he said that, the sound of singing came from inside the church. "I hope you can fix the bell, Tom. We've not dared give it voice since we found a crack in one of the trusses."

"We praise the Lord with more than our music," said Dad, picking up his tool box.

"Then let's climb the tower."

Jenny and I chewed our gum very hard.

The turret of St. Mary's and St. George loomed above us. It soared up into the sky revealing at its top squared notches and a waving white flag with a red cross.

"The parapet," I whispered to Jenny. "Medieval knights could fight up there with swords, or Robin Hood could shoot his bow and arrow." The two of us stared straight up. Then Jenny looked at me very seriously.

Reaching deep into a pocket of his robe, Father Robinson pulled out a big key. He opened a narrow door, which was set into the split-rock foundation of the tower. "To the battlements!" he said, and we followed him into a small musty room filled with choir gowns and hymn books.

The voices of the choir were now loud and clear, and the long rolling waves of the organ seemed just beyond the wall.

"This is the choir changing room," said Father Robinson. "That door leads to the chancel, which includes the altar and choir stalls. That door leads to the nave, where the congregation sits. This," he said pointing up, "is the way to the top."

In the ceiling, there was a trap door. Below it, leaning against the wall, was a wooden ladder, and beside it hanging through a neat round hole, was a thick brown bell rope.

"I'll go first," said Father Robinson. He took an oil lantern from a shelf and stepped up onto the ladder. He opened the trap door, then disappeared into a dark hole. I followed very carefully. Then Jenny. Then my dad, now dressed in his coveralls, carrying his tool box.

"Don't let the darkness scare you," we heard Father Robinson say,

"we'll soon have some light." He struck a match, and our faces lit up. He touched the bright flame to the wick of the lantern and suddenly, stone walls took shape. Bolted to one wall, a rusty ladder vanished mysteriously up into the shadows. Beside it hung the bell rope. "This is the first chamber," said Father Robinson. His voice echoed inside the tower. "And now to the second."

I took a deep breath.

In the second chamber, tall louvered windows allowed thin light to stream in. Through two of the walls, dark yawning openings led to blackness.

"Those are the attics above the channel and the nave. The belfry is up one more flight." Again Father Robinson climbed the creaky ladder and vanished through another trap door.

In the third chamber was the bell. It was huge and black, held in place by a dusty framework of thick oak. The rope that rang it dropped straight down, three stories, into the changing room.

"You see there, Tom?" Father Robinson held up the lantern. "A crack in the bell cage. Do you think you can fix it?"

"I'm sure we can," said Dad. "I've everything we need right here."

"Alleluia!" said Father Robinson. He briskly mounted the ladder. "But, first, I'm sure the children would like to see the view." He pushed up hard on the final trap door, and with a sudden snap, sunlight filled the belfry.

"The top of the castle tower," I whispered, turning to Jenny, and then I realized she had not said one word since we had arrived at the church.

"Here they are," said Father Robinson, lifting his arms in praise. "The great cathedrals of the earth."

Below us, the town spread out like a toy train set, with the mountains all around.

"These great cathedrals with their gates of rock and pavements of cloud." Father Robinson filled his lungs with fresh mountain air.

I looked at Jenny. "I'm not afraid," I announced with relief. But Jenny was holding her hands cupped in front of her.

"There's Old Man Mountain," pointed Father Robinson. "And Tekarra, Cavell and Whistler. And my very favourite – Pyramid. A nine-thousand-foot stone giant, brown and black, and dusted in snow."

Dad pointed across the valley. "And a fine view of Old Fort Point."

"Yes, Our Lord created big mountains and little ones, too."

"Are you holding your courage out in front of you?" I asked Jenny.

"No," she said. "I threw up."

"Oh, Jenny," said my dad. "Are ye all right?"

"I threw up," she repeated, holding out her wet hands. "I'm, I'm sorry."

"Not to worry, Jenny," said Father Robinson. He put his hand on her shoulder. "Just bow your head, my dear, and breathe deeply through your nose."

"There we are. That's better now, isn't it? Here, let me clean your hands." Father Robinson lifted part of his black robe and wiped Jenny's palms. "Not to worry about this old cassock. I'll wash it later. There, there." He smiled at her and she smiled back faintly. She was staring straight at the big cross around Father Robinson's neck, not wanting to look over the edge.

"Tom, I'll take Jenny to the vicarage. Her mother is below with the choir. Edward, you stay here and help your father. There we are, Jenny. I've got you now. We'll take it one step at a time."

In the belfry, my dad took out all the tools he was going to use and laid them out neatly on the dusty floor. He lined up bolts, washers, and pieces of wood. I watched him for a while and then climbed back up into the lofty perch of the parapet. I pretended I was a knight fighting with my sword, and then I was Robin Hood shooting my bow and arrow. I leaned my head and shoulders far out over the parapet and looked straight down. I opened my mouth wide, and with my tongue, pushed out my well-chewed gum. It fell straight down, burying itself in the grass.

"Edward! What are ye doin'? That's not nice."

"I was – there's no one down there."

"That doesn't matter. Come in here!" My dad's head disappeared into the hole, and I followed.

He was now twisting the sharp point of an auger into the hard wood of the bell cage. I watched as thin white shavings curled up.

"Dad, what's a soul?"

He stopped twisting the auger and pulled a white handkerchief from his pocket. Beside him, the black bell's mouth gaped downwards. "Yer soul," he said, mopping his forehead with the handkerchief, "is that part of ye that is everything separate from yer body." He rested one elbow on the bell cage. "It's that part of ye that tells ye how to think and how to feel and what to do." He went back to twisting the auger. "Some people believe yer soul never dies."

"Dad, how come the church has a castle tower?"

He picked up a thick bolt and blew two puffs of air into the hole he had just drilled. "Hundreds of years ago, people came to the church for protection. It made sense that from a high spot ye could see a great way." He shoved the bolt into the hole, tapped it gently with a hammer, and it came out the other side. "And the higher ye are," he said, "the closer ye are to God."

"Because God is in heaven?"

Dad placed a steel washer onto the end of the bolt and twisted a nut on top of it. "Ye learn a lot yerself as ye get older, but it seems all things that are spiritual are expressed in altitudes. We always try to have high morals, and if we're good we go to heaven. We even climb the ladder of success. It seems we're always trying to rise to greater heights."

"Did God create all the mountains in Jasper?"

With a big wrench, he was turning the nut onto the bolt. "God created everything. The mountains, the rivers, the lakes." He twisted the nut tighter. "God created all the people, even the blue sky itself."

"How did God create mountains?"

Now, from below, the muffled voices of the choir lifted up through the three chambers. From above, a bright shaft of sunlight dropped through the trap door.

"Before yer mother bakes a pie, she crimps the edges of the dough with her fingers. That's what God did with certain parts of the earth, to create the mountains and valleys. It happened a long time ago, even before there were dinosaurs."

"But, how?"

"It would be nice to know how God did it, but it is more important to just have faith in the fact that God did."

"So what *are* morals?"

Dad picked up a small hand brush and handed it to me. "Morals are knowin' the difference between what's right and what's wrong. You should always treat people the way ye would like to be treated yerself. Now, let's sweep up and leave the place tidy." With a rag, he started wiping the bell cage.

"But, Dad, why tidy up? No one ever comes here."

He looked at me through the sunlight and floating dust.

"When I was your age, your grandad taught me a poem. It goes like this: *In the elder days of art, builders wrought with greatest care, each minute and unseen part...for God sees everywhere.*" He gave the bell a friendly thump with his fist. "It doesn't matter if the bell is high up, and no one can see it. It doesn't matter if no one ever looks in yer closet. You should still always try to do yer very best."

I started sweeping the floor.

"A wonderful poem, Tom." Father Robinson climbed back up into the belfry. He was dressed now in a long white robe. "I have one more task to perform, up top. Would you like to have a final look?" He lifted his arms and seemed to float through the sunshine. All around him, puffs of golden dust billowed and glittered.

"Go ahead, Edward," said Dad. "I'll finish here."

Back in the parapet, Father Robinson looked carefully all around his feet. "Ah, here it is!" From the sleeve of his robe he pulled a piece of Kleenex. He bent down and picked something up. "Chewing gum!" He held the Kleenex high in the air. "Jenny insisted I pick it up before someone stepped on it."

I hid my face peering over the edge. Far below, people were walking up the path – ladies in floppy hats, men wearing suits and ties – all of them coming to church for the Sunday service.

We were gathered in front of the big brown doors that led into the church; Father Robinson dressed in his formal silk gown, me and my mom and dad, and Jenny and Mr. and Mrs. Trotwood. Mrs. Trotwood was wearing her choir gown, as was Sergeant Gumbrell, who joined us on the steps.

"Mrs. T! Magnus!" said Father Robinson. He folded his hands and bowed slightly in turn to each chorister. "The whole town looks forward with great anticipation to your upcoming performance."

Sergeant Gumbrell stood tall, his gown puffing just a little. "Why, thank you, Father. In five short days, the curtain rises on an event, comparable, I'm sure, to the evening I sang with the great Bing Crosby."

"Are you feeling better?" I whispered to Jenny.

"I'm fine," she said, her confidence recovered. "It was the gum. I ate too much gum."

"I saw it. It was a really big piece."

As Sergeant Gumbrell continued reliving the Bing Crosby evening, Father Robinson cast his eyes to the street. "Oh, heavenly day!" he exclaimed. "It's my friend the Welsh Wizard! Could this be the Road to Damascus?"

Sergeant Gumbrell left Bing Crosby on the steps and went into the church. Now Blue Lightning rolled to a slow stop on the other side of Geikie Street, while above us, Smoky the crow flapped and fluttered down to perch on a stone buttress.

Fraser stepped from the old battered truck, wearing his tweeds, and his brown and white brogues.

"Welcome, Fraser! Nice to see you!"

"You, too, Father Robbie. Still working only one day a week?"

Father Robinson was laughing as Jean and the Blossom sisters appeared from the other side of the truck. The three of them were arm in arm. "Good morning," called Father Robinson. "Good morning to you all."

Kate and Pat were wearing their usual flowery dresses, and each of them sported a flat straw hat. Kate's bore a cluster of plastic fruit and Pat's, a bird. Jean was wearing a beautiful white dress that swished when she walked and a pair of white high-heeled shoes.

"The Welsh Wizard?" asked my dad. "Why do you call him that?"

"Because he is a wizard with a fly line. Because he can coax fish from water in biblical proportion."

"But is he Welsh?"

"Of Welsh descent. From a very well-to-do coal mining family near Cardiff. They say Fraser's father was somewhat of a rebel, though, and left for America before the First World War. Settled in Los Angeles, I believe, and was involved in the early development of motion pictures."

Fraser and the women were walking up the path now.

"A fascinating fellow," said Father Robinson. "Lives to fish, to study Jasper's history, and to advance the reading of Sherlock Holmes. I believe, however, there's still much of the coal miner's blood flowing through his veins."

Father Robinson now offered his hand to Jean. "And to whom do we have the pleasure?" He studied her face.

"This is our friend Jean," said Kate. "She's visiting from the United States."

"Happy to meet you!" said Jean. She peered over her sunglasses and her smile captured everyone. Then her face grew even brighter. "Jenny. Edward. Hi!"

Mrs. Trotwood looked closely at Jean, then put her hand on Jenny's shoulder. She hooked her other arm around Mr. Trotwood's elbow. "You," she said to Jean. "I know who you are."

For a moment, Jean seemed apprehensive. But then she smiled and raised her chin. She placed one hand on her hip.

"Time for church," sniffed Mrs. Trotwood, pulling her husband up the steps. "Come along, Jennifer."

Mr. Trotwood lifted his hat. "Good morning, everyone." And he and his hat disappeared through the door.

From high in the castle tower, the bell started to peal.

Fraser put his hands over his ears. "Bells! Hah!" he said to my dad. "Like bagpipes. Better with a lot of distance and a little sentimentality."

As the bell rang out above the church, Jean took Pat Blossom by the arm. "Time for church, Aunt Pat."

I looked up. The sound of the bell was beautiful.

Just inside the church, Mrs. Trotwood left with Father Robinson to prepare for the service. I whispered again to Jenny, "I don't think your mom likes Jean very much."

We were now in the nave of the church. In front of us, long rows of stiff-backed pews marched like soldiers to the front. The oak battalion was split into two flanks by a blue carpeted aisle. On either side, people sat or kneeled. Everything was still.

"I love walking through these church doors," whispered Kate. "I never come through them without feeling grandeur and fascination." She held tight to my mom's arm. "I step in from the open air, and the scent unfolds inside me like a flower."

Mom looked across the pews through a great white arch that stretched from floor to ceiling. "It's filled with light," she said.

There was sunshine everywhere. It covered the altar and bathed the choir stalls; it sank deep into the carpets and danced on the polished floors. It glinted and gleamed on candle stick and cross.

On every wall, stained glass glistened like coloured ice. Each window told a story: Jesus and the Lamb, Mary and the Child, George and the Dragon.

As we walked down the aisle, Jenny whispered. "See the eagle?"

Below the white arch was a wooden lectern, carved in the perfect shape of an eagle. Its wings were spread, its beak hooked, its eyes were determined.

Now we shuffled, one by one, into the first row on the left-hand side. As we sat down, I glanced over my shoulder. Every head in the church was turned in our direction. My dad stared straight up. "A noble interior," he whispered. "Thick vaulted beams and rafters, all joined together to hold the church in place."

The organ music stopped, and the small door of the choir room opened. A man in a white gown appeared holding a large gold cross in both hands. He smiled as he stepped into the nave followed by the choir members, all lined up in pairs. As they marched into the chancel and their stalls, Father Robinson appeared at the altar. He turned to the congregation. "The Lord be with you," he said cheerfully.

"And with thy spirit," answered the congregation.

"Let us pray!"

We all kneeled on cushioned platforms at our feet.

With her hands clasped, Jenny leaned in my direction. She whispered. "What time do your mom and dad go to bed?"

"What?"

"Your mom and dad – what time do they go to bed?"

"I don't know."

"You don't know?"

"I'm not allowed to stay up that late."

At the altar, Father Robinson was still giving praise to the Lord. Each time he spoke, the congregation responded.

"I believe in one God," said Father Robinson.

"The maker of heaven and earth," said the congregation.

"And of all things visible and invisible."

As the liturgy continued, Jenny kept whispering.

"You don't know what time your mom and dad go to bed?"

"No."

"Well, we have to sneak out."

"Why?"

"We need more clues. There are too many things we don't know. Too many mysteries."

"But Father Robinson said life is full of mystery."

"But don't you want to know where Fraser goes at night? And what happened to Kate and Pat's sister? And who's Tippy? And the man with curly red hair? And what about your mother's letter, Edward? The letter from Aunt Edie? We'll sneak out at midnight."

"Midnight?"

"We'll use the methods of Sherlock Holmes."

"But, I have to be in bed by nine-thirty."

We looked up to see Father Robinson standing below the great white arch. Beside him, the eagle's beady eye was staring straight in our direction.

"Hymn number 392," said Father Robinson loudly. "'Hark, a Thrilling Voice is Sounding.'"

Everyone in the church stood and there was much throat clearing and raising of hymn books. The organ droned deep, dark, puffy notes, and the choir sang with high clear voices.

Hark a thrilling voice is sounding.

The congregation followed – some in, some out of tune.

Christ is nigh, it seems to say.

And now the church was full of music, and from high in the tower, the bell my dad had fixed pealed with merry ringing.

Cast away the dreams of darkness, O ye children of the day!

It was a joyful sound, and it lifted into the rafters. And though I didn't know the meaning of the words, I sang loud and with feeling, and my heart was as full as it could be. The organ boomed its final notes and the voice of the bell drifted into silence. I felt my mom squeeze my hand. It was all very wonderful.

Father Robinson stepped up to the pulpit that was carved like an eagle and bowed his head. When he looked up, he smiled and said, "Dear Lord. We praise you with more than our singing. Help us to be like the builders, who in the elder days of art, wrought with infinite care, each minute and unseen part, for we know that you, dear Lord, can see everywhere."

Jenny pulled at my sleeve. She whispered. "Tonight at midnight, at Mountaintop Rock."

"Midnight? That's pretty late. Should we make it eleven?"

Jenny thought for a moment. "Eleven-thirty."

The eagle was staring straight at us.

Chapter 14

A Musical Chord that Lingers

When the clock by my bed ticked past eleven-thirty, I knew my mom and dad were asleep. In the kitchen, I stepped quietly onto a chair and crawled out the window. The night seemed to be holding its breath. In the cool darkness, I was on the very spot where Mrs. Trotwood had tripped over the bear. My heart pounded.

Up and down the alley, pools of light spilled from back porches. As I stepped carefully through the black, I wondered if more bears were near by rooting for garbage. Somewhere close, I heard the crunch of gravel. I gasped and stepped quickly, then stumbled into the inky shadows of Mountaintop Rock.

"Aaa, Edward," Jenny flapped her hands, then grabbed at my arm.

"Sorry, sorry," I said, "if I scared you." I tried to catch my breath.

"Oh," said Jenny, dropping my arm. "I wasn't scared. Were *you* scared?"

"I was a little bit."

"Oh, I wasn't scared," she said, again. "Sherlock Holmes and Dr.

Watson were never scared when *they* went out at night."

"But they never had bears eating their garbage."

Jenny's smile now shone through the darkness. "It's nice out tonight, though, isn't it? So peaceful – and look at all the stars." She turned her palms into the air, and spun around. "Everything's covered in moonlight."

"I wasn't really scared," I said.

Jenny took her notebook from her pocket and held it up to the light of the moon. She read: "*When you have eliminated all that is impossible, then whatever remains, however improbable, must be the truth.*" She tapped the notebook on her chin. "We've got to use our powers of observation. Hmmm. Where does Fraser go every night? Well, he can't go to the Athabasca Hotel or the Moose's Nook. Surely they're not open late at night."

"Maybe he goes fishing."

"But, why? Why would he go fishing when it's dark? The fish can't see." She nodded thoughtfully. "I think we better look for more clues."

Cautiously, Jenny and I slipped from the shadows and skulked up the alley.

As we crept through the gate in the Blossom sisters' hedge, we heard a strange voice. It was coming from Fraser's garage. It was a man's voice, yet soft and very gentle. He spoke as if telling a story.

"I realized now, more clearly than ever," said the man, "the great loss the world had sustained by the death of Sherlock Holmes."

In the darkness, Jenny's eyes were wide. "Dr. Watson!"

As we tiptoed along the path, we could see that the garage door was ajar, and a shaft of light splashed out across the book barrel. The man telling the story was still speaking as Jenny and I bowed our heads, and knelt beside all the books.

"I had not been in my study for five minutes," continued the story-teller, "when the maid entered to say a person desired to see me. To my astonishment, it was none other than the old bookseller, his sharp, wiz-ened face peering out from a frame of white hair, his precious volumes, a dozen of them at least, wedged under his right arm."

Then from the shaft of light through the open door, there came another voice. It was dry and crackly. It was the voice of the old book-seller.

"You're surprised to see me, sir," he croaked. "If it isn't too great a liberty, I am a neighbour of yours. You'll find my little book shop at the corner of Church Street."

Jenny and I huddled closer to the book barrel. She whispered into to my ear. "They have British accents, Edward, like yours."

The bookseller then said to the storyteller, "These volumes are a bargain, sir. With five of them, you could fill that gap on the second shelf. It looks untidy, does it not?"

Then the storyteller spoke with great emotion. "I moved my head to look at the shelf! And when I turned back, there was Sherlock Holmes standing smiling at me. I rose to my feet, stared at him for some seconds in utter amazement. Then it appears, for the first and last time in my life, I fainted. Grey mist swirled before my eyes."

Jenny's face lifted up into the light as we heard yet another man's voice, this one strong and full of authority. "My dear Watson! I owe you a thousand apologies! I had no idea you would be so affected."

"Holmes," cried the storyteller. "Is it really you?"

"Sherlock Holmes– " said Jenny.

Suddenly Fraser's garage was filled with clapping.

"Bravo! Bravo!" shouted a woman.

"Jean!" exclaimed Jenny.

"Hurrah! Hurrah!" shouted Jean, from inside the garage.

And then amidst all of Jean's clapping and cheering, another voice that Jenny and I recognized yelled, "Thank you! Thank you very much!"

"Bravo! Fraser!" laughed Jean. "You can still do it! You can still bring Sherlock and all the characters back to life."

Fraser was laughing. "It's in my blood, Jean. Acting is in my blood!"

Suddenly the door opened wide and the yard was filled with light. Fraser and Jean stood in the doorway, their shadows draped across the lawn.

"We'd better deliver these before we head down the road," said Jean. In her hand were four glistening trout, dangling from a piece of cut willow.

"I'll just chuck this in the garbage."

As Fraser carried something wrapped in newspaper to the alley, Jenny and I shrunk deeper into the shadow of the barrel. Jean switched out the light, and the two of them went laughing up the steps into the back porch.

"They must have gone fishing already," I whispered.

"But they're going somewhere," said Jenny. "Jean said they were heading down the road."

From the house, we heard Kate Blossom's voice. "Jean. Fraser.

Come in! How nice." The door into the kitchen closed, and there was silence.

Jenny's fingers gripped my arm. "We've got to get closer."

Now she was tiptoeing towards the back steps. "Edward, come on."

Somewhere up the alley a dog barked.

As Jenny slowly pulled open the screen door, it squeaked. She looked back. "Shhh…!"

The porch was now cloaked in darkness. The armchairs and the old radio were black holes full of dreadful things. The flowers in the vase were drooped and wilted, and all around us, the mosquito screen dulled the moonlight.

I tried to swallow. "I'm a little bit scared now," I said.

Jenny stepped further into the darkness. From the other side of the kitchen door, Kate's voice was clear.

"Let's have a nice cup of tea before you go."

Then we heard the soft clatter of teacups.

"Where's Pat?" asked Jean.

"She'll be back soon," Kate said. "She's still looking for – " the shrill whistle of the kettle covered her words. Jenny and I leaned forward straining our ears.

"She wanders so much, now, in her body, and her mind. I'm so worried about her. Her memory – so muddled – and she does everything wrong."

Kate's voice became even shakier.

"I know I shouldn't, but sometimes I get angry at her."

Suddenly Kate was crying. "I know it's not her fault."

"But it's not your fault either, Aunt Kate," said Jean.

"And I'm angry, angry with God!" Kate sobbed. "Angry that this has happened. "Her voice died to a whisper. "A lifetime of memories, and no one to share them with – as she goes away."

In the porch, the darkness deepened. The numbing silence went on till Fraser said, "Give us a smile, Kate, and we'll have a nice cup of tea." Then we heard again the sound of the teacups.

When the kitchen door opened, a bolt of yellow light dropped across the floor. Jenny and I stepped back deeper into the shadows.

Kate was smiling now. "You two be careful tonight." She kissed Fraser and Jean before they went down the steps.

Jenny and I were alone once more in the porch. We listened as Blue Lightning awoke and rumbled down the alley to its mysterious nightly mission.

As she turned in the darkness, I heard a bump behind me. I felt a terrible knot in my stomach. Then, there was a noise like a popgun. A light flashed and Jenny's face lit up. She screamed. The light went out with a crash, and I spun around. Beside the radio was a dark figure. The light flashed again, and I saw the face of a horrible creature. Again Jenny screamed.

"I dropped it," said a voice. "I dropped the flashlight."

"Pat?"

The kitchen door flew open. "Pat! There you are. And, my goodness, Jenny and Edward. What are you doing up so late?"

"We…were out," said Jenny.

"Out?" said Kate smiling. "Well then, would you like to come in?"

Jenny was catching her breath. She stared at Pat.

"Come in! Come in, children," Kate said. "Come and see the lovely trout that Fraser and Jean caught for us."

On the kitchen wall above the sink, the black cat's plastic tail still swung back and forth, its eyes looked from side to side.

As Kate helped Pat off with her cardigan, I paid close attention to the four trout, now on a platter, on the counter. Their heads were still attached, but they had slits up their bellies, and their insides had been taken out.

"Are you going to eat these trout?" I asked.

"We're going to fry them in butter tomorrow morning for breakfast." Kate gave Pat's cardigan a shake out the kitchen door. "Have you ever had trout before, Edward?"

"Never."

"Never had pan fried trout with oven fresh bread and sliced tomatoes, drenched in vinegar and olive oil? My goodness! What a pity." She hung the cardigan in the closet. "Well, these trout are cleaned and ready

for the pan. But, do your parents know you're out this late?"

"Oh," said Jenny confidently, "we're allowed to come and see you anytime."

"Ah, well, then." Kate smiled. "Our daddy used to say, 'Never pass up a chance for adventure.' Shall we fry the trout tonight?"

"Yes, please!" I said.

Kate took her sister by the arm. "Come, my dear. Let's fill the tub, and you can have a nice hot soak. Edward, turn on the radio, please, and we'll have some music."

When Kate returned to the kitchen, steam was drifting down the hallway as hot water splashed into the tub. Classical music was playing on the radio.

"Perfect for a summer night," said Kate, "Mendelssohn's *Overture to A Midsummer Night's Dream.*" She twisted the top from a silver canister and lifted out a handful of white flour.

"*If we shadows have offended,*" she looked at us with a mysterious smile, and her eyes twinkled. "*Think but this and all is mended,*" her fingers danced above the trout, showering them with flour dust. "*That you have only slumbered here. While these visions did appear.*" She turned the trout over, coating them in the flour. "That's from a play by William Shakespeare."

"He was a writer, too, wasn't he?" asked Jenny.

Kate shook salt and pepper all over the trout. "Someone once said, Shakespeare was the poet who, after God, created the most. Even Sir Arthur Conan Doyle didn't write as much as Shakespeare." With two hands, she lifted a black skillet onto the stove.

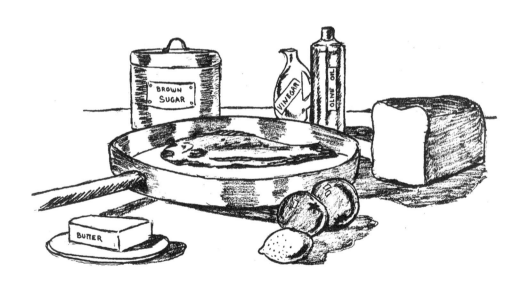

"How come sometimes Pat can't remember things?" asked Jenny.

Kate thought for a moment. She turned a knob on the stove and a purple flame popped up.

"Sometimes, Jenny, when you get older, parts of your body don't work as well as they used to." With a table knife, she dolloped thick curls of butter into the pan.

"But sometimes she *can* remember."

"Sometimes she can. Sometimes she remembers things that I have forgotten – things from our childhood." The butter in the pan started to bubble gently. "Sometimes she's happy, and sometimes she's sad." One by one, Kate picked up each trout by its tail and placed it into the bubbles. "Sometimes she gets angry, and sometimes she laughs."

"Does she ever cry?"

"She does, sometimes. She seems to change horses, right in the middle of the stream."

The butter in the skillet now smoked and Kate adjusted the flame. "We must always remember to keep an even heat, so that the butter is always hot, but never turns brown, and we must never let the trout dry out or get too brown on the bottom."

She took three plump tomatoes from a bowl on the counter and washed them under running water.

"Edward, take the spatula, please, and check to see that the fish aren't burning." She sliced tomatoes on a cutting board. "And here, Jenny, pour olive oil over these. That's right, dear, the green bottle. It came all the way from Europe. I'll set the table."

Mendelssohn's overture drifted about the kitchen as Jenny drizzled oil onto the tomatoes, and I looked under the fish. Down the hallway in the bathroom, Pat was still soaking in the tub.

"Kate, what happened to your sister, Winnifred?"

From outside there came a sound like a distant clap of thunder. Up the alley a garbage can had been tipped.

"Sounds like we're not the only ones having a midnight snack." With one hand on her cane, Kate used her free hand to finish placing knives and forks on the table. She sat down. "You asked about

Winnifred." Her eyes were drawn to the dark window. "Winnie likes to win. That's what Daddy used to say. He'd laugh and pat her on the head. 'Our Winnie always likes to win.'"

Kate leaned her cane gently against the table. "There were three of us, three little girls. I was born first, then a year later came Pat. It was five years before Winnie was born, while we were in Edmonton." Kate spoke softly, smiling to herself. "Such a long time ago. They called us the Three Musketeers."

I caught a glance from Jenny.

"We were three children from a loving family, treated equally with kindness and respect. And yet," she added with a tender expression, "and yet, Winnie was never like Pat and me. She had no interest in painting. She was always dressing up, always performing. She liked to mimic, to imitate. She lived in the world of her imagination: always inventing disguises, but always wanting the lion's share of the attention.

"When Daddy went to fight the war in Africa, Mother took us back to England, and while Pat and I attended art classes, Winnie was enrolled in the Royal School of Drama. Then when Pat and I travelled Europe with our easels and our paint boxes, Winnie found small parts on the London stage. And when she wasn't acting in plays, she was writing them. Winnie loved to make up stories. She was such a beautiful girl, green eyes and long dark hair. She always found a way to get what she wanted.

"When we were in our twenties, we three decided to come back to Canada. We travelled together, but in many ways, Winnie was never with us. She always did things by herself, or with the friends that she made, or, or maybe it was Pat and I. Maybe *we* were different. All the same, the three of us decided to stay in Jasper, and make the mountains our home.

"One day in the summer of 1915, Pat and I were walking out to Tent City. It was a beautiful morning. We had heard they were looking for women to work as chars at the new camp resort. We crossed the wooden bridge at Old Fort Point and started down the road towards Lac Beauvert. Suddenly, without warning, a huge horse galloped from the trees. The man riding the horse didn't see us. I was knocked down and trampled beneath its hooves. My leg was broken badly, and I spent the rest of that summer in the doctor's shack in Jasper. There was no hospital here in those days."

"Was the man sorry?" asked Jenny.

Kate thought for a moment. "For about a week after the accident, the man on the horse came with Pat to see me every day. He was a charming man, very debonair. He was a guest at Tent City. By then, Pat was a char girl, and he courted her every day. She was very fond of him. He had a camera, and he made motion pictures."

"Was he Pat's boyfriend?"

"For a short while he was. But Winnie arranged for a job as a char girl, too, and by the end of the summer, by the time I was up and about, the man had turned his attention to her. Soon they were very much in love. When I went out one day to visit Pat at Tent City, we stood on the shores of Lac Beauvert as Winnie and the man went by in a horse drawn carriage. We followed them as they went through the trees and around the lake. When we got to the bay by the 14th tee, Winnie turned and waved. Then they just drove away. It sounds silly, I know, and very dramatic, but I was left with a broken leg, and Pat with a broken heart. We never saw Winnie again."

Kate rested her weight on the cane and stood up. "Turn the trout over now, please, Edward or they'll be too brown on the bottom."

"Where did Winnie and the man go?"

"To Los Angeles, California."

"Los Angeles," repeated Jenny, her eyes wide. Now she was the great detective. "Jean is from Los Angeles."

Kate opened the door of the oven and put four plates inside to warm. "Tent City was most successful that summer. Lots of people came from all over the world. But it closed immediately following its first season. Now the world was at war, the Great War, World War One."

Kate poured glasses of cold milk. "Our poor daddy had died by then. We learned of Winnie's affairs only through our mother's letters."

"What happened to Winnie?"

"Winnie's husband was a film director in Hollywood."

"Her husband?"

Yes, they were married, and for some years led an exciting life. They drove motor cars and had fancy parties. Winnie even acted in some films. The nineteen twenties were called the Jazz Age. It was a wonderful time. The war was over and everyone thought the fun and prosperity would last forever. But when the thirties began, good times turned to hard times, and so did Winnie's marriage. Now there was a child, and life was not as glittery as it had been. Her husband, David, left her."

"Her husband's name was David?"

"David Gareth McKillop."

"McKillop?"

"He was Fraser's father."

"Then, you're Fraser's aunt?"

"I am."

With a sharp knife, Kate now cut a big yellow lemon into four pieces. With her spatula, she inspected each of the fish. "Perfect," she said. "Golden brown!"

"Jean calls you Aunt, too," said Jenny.

"It was the Dirty Thirties. Winnie and her son Fraser now lived right in the heart of the glamorous film industry, but there was little money. They had to stay in rented rooms and apartments. Winnie found no more acting jobs, so she became a film cutter for a big studio. Her job was splicing films together. Fraser was 12 years old then. He was going to a school in Hollywood. Every day on his way to school, he would see a little girl with her dog. The dog always followed the girl and waited for her in the playground, and when school was over, she and the dog would walk home together."

Kate squeezed lemon above the fish. The juice drizzled onto the trout, and the skillet sizzled.

"But the little dog barked a lot, and one day an angry neighbour took a gun and shot it."

"Shot the dog?" Jenny's face twisted with pain. "How could anyone shoot a dog?"

"Fraser rushed to the girl's rescue. He picked up the dog and walked with the girl to her house, where she lived with her mother."

"Was the girl Jean?" asked Jenny.

"Yes, the girl was Jean. Her mother's name was Gladys, and like Winnie, she too had no husband. Winnie and Gladys became friends, and after the dog was buried, the two mothers and their children lived together in the same house."

"On Arbol Drive!" deduced Jenny.

"That's right, Arbol Drive."

"What was the dog's name?"

"The dog's name was Tippy."

The music on the radio was now quiet and dreamy. "That's a very sad story," I said.

"It is a sad story, but there are lots of sad stories in life. Our daddy used to say that you have to strive to be happy. He said that your brain is like a muscle, and you can exercise it; you can make it strong and happy, or you let it get weak and sad. 'Work hard at being happy,' he used to say, 'Exercise your brain!'"

Kate opened another silver canister and dipped into it with a teaspoon. She held the spoon above the skillet and sprinkled brown sugar all over the trout. The sugar bubbled, and now the music was bright and cheery.

"I've made observations," said Jenny, holding her notebook. "I've got more questions."

"Well then, my dear Holmes, you better ask them."

"When did Fraser come to Jasper? And what do Fraser and Jean do for a living?"

"When the Great Depression came in the thirties, the economic system collapsed all over the world. In Hollywood, Winnie and Gladys were both out of work, and Winnie was too proud to ask for help from our family. Gladys became sick, and had to go to a special home. And, sadly, Jean had to live in an orphanage. As Fraser grew older, Winnie seemed to lose interest in being a mother, and after several years of coming to the mountains for his school holidays, Fraser decided to live with Pat and me here in Jasper."

"Did Jean still live in the orphanage?"

"She did. But she was a very pretty girl, and as soon as she was old enough, she quit school to become a photographer's model. Her picture was on all the magazine covers during the Second World War. That's when she began to visit us, when she started thinking of us as family."

"She was on magazine covers," said Jenny, looking at me, and nodding with respect.

"What was Fraser's job when he came to Jasper?" I asked.

Kate tipped the skillet and touched each of the golden trout with her spatula. "Fraser always called himself a pitman. He would laugh and say, 'Digging runs deep in my veins!' His ancestors on his father's side were coal miners in Wales, so when Fraser came to live with us, he took a job in the mine at Cadomin, up at the Coal Branch. Cadomin is one of the towns that produce coal for the railway. But Fraser could see the coming change in technology, and he knew that eventually the big locomotives would run on diesel rather than steam. Not long after that, he came into his inheritance."

"Did he become rich?"

"I would be lying, Jenny, if I were to say that members of our family were not born with silver spoons in their mouths."

"Are you and Pat rich, too?"

"We have what we need. But when our nephew Fraser took residency in our garage, we felt truly blessed – as if we'd been given a son." Kate gazed into the skillet. "We told Fraser all the things his grandfather had told us: how you can hold your courage in the palm of your hand; how you should never be afraid to take a chance. And when Pat and I went into the hills with our paint boxes and our easels, Fraser and his fishing rod were always with us. We showed him the beauty of the mountains and told him the great unfolding story of the Athabasca Valley. Soon his soul turned to the tales of David Thompson and William Henry. We told him of our family friendship with Sir Arthur Conan Doyle, and his mind became intoxicated with the mysteries and adventures of the Great Detective."

Kate was now lost in her own story, sharing her memories with the tick-tock of the clock on the wall and the gentle music that wreathed the room.

"And as the seasons turned," she said, "in weather fair or foul, Fraser's head was filled with the most wondrous thoughts. While he walked by a stream or floated on a high alpine lake, his mind was embroidered with the magic of the mountains and the enchanted stories of Sherlock Holmes." She touched each of the golden trout again with the spatula, and again the skillet sizzled. "All the clues and the characters, the adventures and the mystery, the excitement, it all swept together in his mind, and stayed like a musical chord that lingers. And I am certain that his childhood friend, was never far from his mind."

"Jean," said Jenny.

Kate gripped the handle of her cane and turned to look at the watercolours on the wall. "The vision of a young man's love," she said softly, "is surpassed by no future splendour. And the first glory of a mountain view never comes again."

"There were hundreds of twinkling lights." We looked to the entrance of the hallway. Pat was there in her pink dressing gown and bedroom slippers. She seemed confused. "Hundreds of twinkling lights," she said again, "round and round, all the names up there," she pointed to the ceiling, "in the twinkling lights."

"Whose names?" asked Jenny.

"Pat, did you have a nice bath?" Kate took her sister's hand and led her to the table. "Let's have our supper now."

Pat stared at Jenny and me, as if we were strangers.

"These are our friends, Pat," Kate said. "Our friends, Jenny and Edward. We're having trout. You remember. The trout Fraser and Jean caught."

"Was it Winnie's name in the twinkling lights?" asked Jenny.

Kate took warm plates from the oven and placed them on the counter. "No, it wasn't Winnie's name, Jenny. When we took the train to Edmonton, it was Jean's name we saw in the lights."

"Jean's?"

Kate placed one trout on each of the four plates and squeezed on more lemon juice.

"You remember, Pat. We went to the city and stood below the big marquee on 101 St. The night sky was dark, but the sign was bright, and all the snowflakes drifted down among the twinkling lights, and Jean's name was there."

"Why?" asked Jenny.

"Jean is in the movies."

"In cowboy movies?" I asked.

"Not the kind you see on Saturday afternoon, Edward. The kind your parents go to."

"Is she famous?"

"Very famous."

"Why doesn't my mom like her?" asked Jenny.

Kate now brought the plates to the table. Next to each trout, she placed sliced tomatoes and a big piece of fresh bread. I took the smells of the kitchen into my nose, and then cut into the trout with my knife. On the outside, it was crisp and golden brown; inside, it was pink and flaky moist. In my mouth it was delicious.

"Fried trout tastes like a summer evening," said Kate. "It brings back such happy memories." She smiled across the table. "It's even better by a campfire, among the pines. Try some vinegar on your fish, Edward."

"People think she's a hussy," Pat said.

"A hussy," said Jenny. "A hussy?"

"But she's not a hussy," said Kate.

With a piece of bread, I soaked up juice from the fish and oil from the tomatoes. With my fingers, I squished it into a ball, and popped it into my mouth.

"What is a hussy?" asked Jenny

Kate dashed vinegar onto her trout. "A woman who is bold and mischievous."

"Bold," said Jenny. "Like a hoyden? Or a tomboy?"

"Your mother is only trying to protect you, Jenny."

"Daddy said let your morals be your guide," said Pat.

"Maybe Jean doesn't know the difference between right and wrong," I said, with a mouth full of bread.

"Jean is a reflection of our times," said Kate. "In many ways she is ahead of it. She has a way of making people see themselves. She loves life and beauty, and she has an open heart." Kate lifted a small forkful of fish to her mouth. "We should look *into* people, as well as at them."

"Maybe Jean helps people to feel like it's their own names up in the twinkling lights," said Jenny.

Pat had now eaten everything on her plate, leaving just a white skeleton of a fish, with its head and tail attached. Jenny had only picked at a small portion of her trout, but had eaten everything else, except for a slice of tomato, which she used to cover the fish's head.

"Why is it such a big secret that Jean is in Jasper?" Jenny asked.

"Our Jean is here only for a short time," said Kate, "and too many people want to talk to the other Jean or take her picture or ask for an autograph." Kate glanced at Pat as Pat stood up. "Our Jean will be leaving on the train the day after tomorrow."

"For Los Angeles?" asked Jenny.

"No, for New York."

"The Indian people," murmured Pat. She was now standing below the black cat clock. "The Indian people believed that if you had your picture taken…"

"…the camera stole your soul," finished Jenny. The music on the radio drifted away gently, as though into a dark forest. "Do you know where Fraser goes every night, Pat?"

A long hollow gong sounded from the alley, and a tiny shiver went through the kitchen. Outside, a barrel had tipped, and a bear was feeding.

"I wonder if we should go home pretty soon," I said.

Kate stood up. "Well, it's been a lovely evening, hasn't it, Pat? I'll walk the children across the alley, and then it's time for bed."

"The trout was delicious," I said. "Thank you."

As we said good night to Pat, Kate flipped a switch on the porch wall and light streamed into the yard. It stopped abruptly at the hedge.

We went down the steps. As we approached the black hole that was the gate, we heard a snuffing, shuffling sound. As Kate peered into the alley a loud snort erupted, and a barrel rolled and, with a sound like scattering gravel, a huge furry animal shot past. Its eyes were bright in the light from the porch; a piece of shredded newspaper was dangling from its mouth.

Kate's arms shot out. "It's all right. He's on his way."

Jenny and I stuck our heads into the alley. The black bear ran with great speed, but then suddenly slowed to a sluggish stroll and looked back. Calmly it disappeared into the shadows of Mountaintop Rock.

"We won't see him again," said Kate. "There's lots for him to eat down the alley." She took us both by the hand.

Standing at our back gate, Kate smiled. "Well, you must go in the way you came out, and if there are consequences, you'll just have to face up to them." She put her arms around us. "Good night, my dears." Then she hugged us and walked back across the alley.

"Kate," whispered Jenny.

"Yes, dear."

"I hope Pat gets better."

"Thank you, Jenny."

"And, Kate?"

"Yes?"

"Where *does* Fraser go at night?"

For a moment I thought Kate had gone, but her voice came out of the darkness. "Sometimes I think he's a man who's looking for himself."

"For himself?"

"I'm sure we're all digging around somewhere, Jenny, searching for ourselves, or something, or someone."

"Digging," Jenny whispered.

"Good night, children."

The black night now wrapped itself around everything. I turned and stared into the darkness to see if there were any bears lying across our path.

When we reached the house, I asked Jenny why she didn't eat her trout.

"I couldn't," she said. "I just couldn't. It was staring at me. I'll see you in the morning, Edward." Then she slipped silently through the back door.

Holding my breath, I tiptoed around the corner, and crawled in through the kitchen window.

CHAPTER 15

LOST AND FOUND

The next morning Jean was running up and down the alley, wearing a sweatsuit. With her long dark hair flowing behind her, she dashed to where Jenny and I were sitting on Mountaintop Rock.

"Hi!" she said, lifting her sunglasses to her forehead. "It's a beautiful morning!" She was running in place now, her knees pumping up and down.

"Are you practising for a race?" asked Jenny.

"No. This is how I stay in shape, how I keep fit."

"By running?"

"I'm not sure I'd call it running, sweetie. I just kind of jog myself about and shake my parts a bit."

"Could we jog with you?"

Jean laughed. "I've never heard it called that before, but I'm sure you could. Come on!"

Jenny and I jogged with Jean up the alley, shaking about and flopping our hands in the air. Jean was quick, so we had to move fast.

"Are you a good friend of Fraser's?" asked Jenny.

"Yes. I am."

"Have you known him for a long time?"

"I have."

"Your husband, is he coming to Jasper?"

Jean didn't answer, so I thought I should ask a question.

"Do you like fishing and books?"

Jean stopped, but her knees were still pumping. "I like fishing. And since you ask, I also like books. In fact, my husband is in a book, and the book is about a man who catches a big fish."

Jenny and I were running in place, our legs flying and our elbows flapping.

"Was your husband the man who caught the big fish?" I asked between breaths.

"No. The great fish was caught by an old man, but once he had caught it, he had to protect it from sharks that wanted to eat it. It's a wonderful story about honour, courage, and grace under pressure."

"Did the old man stop the sharks from eating the fish?"

Jean started back down the alley. "When I get home to Los Angeles, I'll send you a copy, and you can find out for yourself."

We were huffing and puffing as we approached the Blossom sisters' gate.

"Do you know where Fraser goes every night?" Jenny asked. "And do you know...."

Jean stopped. She smiled and, with the back of her hand, brushed Jenny's cheek. "You two guys are my new favourite sweethearts," she touched the end of my nose with the tip of her finger, "but you ask a lot of questions." Then she lifted the bottom of her sweatshirt and wiped her forehead. I could see her belly, and the more I stared, the nicer it looked.

"I'm guessing you were both up very late last night." Jean wagged her finger. "And for your information, my husband is *not* coming to Jasper." She dug deep into the pocket of her sweatpants. "Jenny, maybe you'd like to have this." She handed Jenny the rusty paint box that we had found in the tunnel. "And Edward, I believe this is yours." It was the airmail letter from Aunt Edie.

Jean smiled her big beautiful smile, then ran into the Blossom sisters' yard. I ran home as fast as I could to ask my mom if I should check the mail.

Chapter 16

A Legacy

Jenny and I were up early. Mrs. Trotwood and Sergeant Gumbrell were practising.

Overnight, there had been rain, and when the sun came out we climbed onto Mountaintop Rock and watched Smoky the crow make mud puddle soup. With wings flapping, he flipped slices of stale bread into a puddle, and then hopping up and down like he was on a pogo stick, waited for it to soak right through.

"I think he's full," said Jenny. "Shall we go play tag at the totem pole?"

We wandered down the alley, through the garbage the bears had scattered the night before, turned right at the Texaco onto Connaught, and headed for the train station.

"The Trans Continental is in," I said. "And look. There's the gum machine."

On the crowded platform, we spotted a blue uniform and shiny buttons. Sergeant Gumbrell was marching about staring at all the passengers.

"He's got his sheet music," said Jenny. "Hi Sergeant Gumbrell! Are you looking for your friend?"

"I am. I'm hoping to tell her about our big concert next weekend. I'm certain she would enjoy it. She's going to be a school teacher, you know." He kept looking at all the faces.

"Do you want your friend to stay?"

Sergeant Gumbrell straightened his shoulders and his tunic stretched across his chest. "I do."

"All aboard!" shouted the conductor, and the passengers started to board the train.

Now, Sergeant Gumbrell stood tall and proud on the station platform. As each big green car glided by, he stared into its window. When the final car passed and the soft click-clack sound started to fade, he turned to Jenny and me like he was going to share a secret.

"Sometimes," he whispered, "sometimes you meet someone, and you just know." He tried to smile, as he reached into his pocket and drew out the white paper bag.

"She's a lovely lady," he said sadly. "We only spoke briefly, but something about her touched me that night." He looked down at the paper bag in his hand; it was empty.

The alley was dry and the sun was shining as Jenny and I walked home, dragging sticks along all the picket fences.

"I wonder what movies Jean has been in," I said. "Maybe some with Randolph Scott."

As we approached Fraser's garage, we stopped to throw stones in the air and hit them with our sticks. Then, we took turns kicking the stones until we came to the Blossom sisters' gate.

"Who's that?" asked Jenny.

Sitting cross-legged on the lawn by the fountain was a woman with shiny blonde hair. She was wearing a pink fuzzy sweater and blue jeans.

"Jenny! Edward! Hi! Come help me build the kite." In one hand, the woman held a pair of scissors; in the other, a large, diamond-shaped frame made of very thin wood. The frame was partly covered with sheets of white paper. Beside her in a neat pile were more sheets of paper and a glue pot with a small brush sticking out.

"It's Jean!" said Jenny. We ran into the yard. "You look *different*."

Jean smiled and sat up straight. Her lips were brighter, and her whole body seemed softer than before. Her hair, which yesterday had been brown and straight, was now blonde, in soft wavy curls.

"You look like an angel," Jenny determined.

"An angel," laughed Jean. "No one's ever called me that before." She

placed her hands on her hips. "But I'm still me. How do you think I look, Edward?" She tossed her head back, and her hair bounced around her shoulders.

I stared at her. "You look beautiful. Very beautiful." But somehow she was more than beautiful. She looked powerful, too – like if she wanted to, she could save all the settlers in Missouri or find the lost gold in California. In my mind I couldn't describe her beauty exactly, but I couldn't take my eyes from her face. Everything about her made me feel warm and good. I just wanted to stare. "You look powerful," I said.

"Powerful!" She laughed, clicking the big scissors together. "Well, I've heard gentlemen prefer blondes."

I kept staring at her, and at that moment there was nothing more important in the world than helping Jean build that kite.

"You're in Hollywood movies," said Jenny.

"I am," confirmed Jean, picking up a sheet of paper from the pile beside her. She used the small brush to carefully wipe the edges with glue. "Have you seen any of my films?"

"I don't think so," said Jenny.

Jean filled an empty space on the frame with the paper.

"Have you been in any movies with Randolph Scott?" I asked, handing her another sheet.

"No. But I know Randy Scott."

"Randy? You call him Randy?"

"He's a very nice man."

I looked at Jenny in astonishment. "She knows *Randy Scott!*"

Jenny was watching carefully as Jean dabbed on more glue. "What are these pages? They have typing on them."

"It's a script for a movie. The pages I'm pasting onto the kite are directions for one particular scene. But I don't need a script for what they want me to do."

"What do they want you to do?"

Jean filled in the final space on the frame and then carefully folded a section of paper that stuck over the edge. She trimmed away the extra paper with the scissors. They were sharp and made a pleasant solid sound as they cut.

"They want me to stand on a subway grate and have the wind blow my dress up in the air."

"Blow your dress in the air," said Jenny. She looked at me, then back at Jean. "So they can – see your underpants?"

"Are you going to do that?" I asked.

Jean looked at us now as if she were a little girl. Her eyes were beautiful.

"I am," she said, "But it's not wicked and shameful, or shocking and dirty. It's funny. It's a comic scene."

Her voice turned to a whisper. "To become a dramatic actress you have to play many parts. Maybe I'm just playing all the bad ones first. I don't want to be what I am now forever. I don't want to be remembered as a glamour queen or a calendar girl."

"Sir Arthur Conan Doyle didn't want to be what he was either," said Jenny. "He didn't want to be remembered for just creating Sherlock Holmes."

"He was a great writer," said Jean. She held the kite high in the air. "He had more than two sides – and so do I. One day I'm going to play Grushenka from the Brothers Karamazov or Princess Cordelia from King Lear."

From a pocket in her blue jeans, Jean pulled out a long piece of string. She picked up another page of the script and scrunched it together in the middle. She tied it onto the piece of string, and then did the same with another page, and another and another, until she made a long kite tail. She tied the tail onto the kite and handed it to me.

"Isn't it great to be alive!" she said, jumping up. She took a deep breath. "The mountain air. When I breathe it in, I'm not afraid of anything."

"You're afraid of things?"

"Sometimes I am."

"What are you afraid of?"

"I'm afraid of not being loved."

"Not being loved? By whom?"

"By everybody."

The screen door slammed. "Ladies and gentlemen," shouted Fraser as he came down the steps. "With great pleasure I now present," he lifted one arm majestically towards the door, "the Blossom sisters!"

The screen door opened and Pat stood at the top of the steps. She was wearing a long, white flowing dress, with lace on the front, and a small bunch of roses pinned to her belt. Her face was made up with powder and lipstick, and she had a fancy hairdo with flips and curls and long white ribbons.

"You look lovely," cried Jean.

Fraser escorted Pat down the steps.

"And Kate!"

Kate Blossom was now in the doorway, supporting herself with her cane. She too wore a long white gown with ruffled shoulders and lots of lace. She wore lipstick, and her cheeks were rosy red.

"Ah, Kate, you're a shining diamond." Fraser kissed Kate and Pat on their foreheads. "You look like movie stars!"

Suddenly another figure appeared behind the screen door.

"The man," said Jenny, nudging me. "It's the man."

"What?"

"The man with curly red hair," she said between clenched teeth.

The screen door opened.

"Jimmy! Come and meet Jenny and Edward," Jean called happily.

The man with curly red hair smiled as he stepped down onto the lawn. In one hand, he carried a long brush and some pencils. In the other hand, a small leather case.

"Hi, there. Nice to see you again."

Jean was beaming. "My good friend Jimmy Herron, meet Jenny and Edward. Jimmy's the best make-up man in Hollywood. He's come all the way from California to help me get ready for my trip to New York."

"Hah!" said Fraser, slapping Jimmy on the back. "And I thought you were a reporter."

"Not me," said Jimmy. "I can keep a secret." He dabbed Kate's cheek softly with one of his brushes. "You look stunning, my dear, just stunning."

"Well," said Fraser. "Let's fly this kite!"

"Yes!" said Jean. "We'll fly the kite from the top of Old Fort Point."

"That would be a bit of a climb for Pat and me," Kate said.

"And I think I've had enough running around," said Jimmy. He was stroking Pat's eyebrow lightly with a thick brown pencil. His head tilted as he looked deep into her eyes. "Perfect," he said. "You look perfect."

"Can we search for the location of Henry House when we get to Old Fort Point?" asked Jenny. She took out her notebook with its list of unanswered questions. "Will you show us where William Henry built his fort in 1811?"

"Well...."

Jean smiled. "The game's afoot, Sherlock. Now you can finally show us the location." She hugged Jenny. "We're going to have such fun!"

"Jennifer, come home now, please. It's time for lunch." Mrs. Trotwood was at the gate.

Jean's arm dropped from Jenny's shoulder.

"But Mom, we're going to fly the kite from the top of Old Fort Point." She picked up the kite and ran towards her mom. But before she reached the gate, she tripped and fell.

Mrs. Trotwood and Jimmy Herron both rushed to Jenny. Jimmy got there first and helped her up. "There you are, Angel Face," he said. "Nothing damaged."

He smiled at Mrs. Trotwood. "Hello. I'm Jim Herron, from L.A. You were singing this morning. You have a lovely voice."

Mrs. Trotwood reached for Jenny's hand. "Thank you."

"Please, Mom, can I go to Old Fort Point?"

"Jennifer, no. I've made lunch."

Jean was by them now. She bent down and picked up the kite. "Honoria, we could all have lunch together?"

Mrs. Trotwood was hesitant. She looked to Kate.

"We've made lots," said Kate, smiling.

"The more the merrier," said Fraser. "Let's all have lunch!"

Jean reached out and touched Mrs. Trotwood's arm. "You and I could talk about singing."

"We could," said Mrs. Trotwood. "I guess we could." She let go of Jenny's hand. "Go to the house, please Jennifer, and bring the sandwiches. They're on the kitchen table. And Edward, you will need permission, too."

Permission was granted all around. We were going to Old Fort Point.

When lunch was finished and the table cleared, Fraser brought his best fishing rod with the silver reel from the garage. He tied the big white kite to the end of its line. "From the top," he said, "you'll be able to see it for miles. Let's go."

As Fraser, Jean, and Jenny were heading for the gate, I stood looking up at Old Fort Point. From the back porch I heard someone call my name. I peered through the screen. "Pat?"

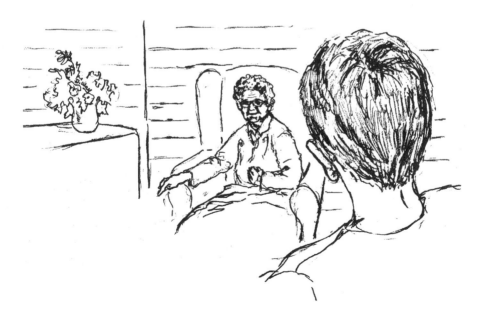

I went up the steps. From the kitchen, I could hear Mrs. Trotwood and Jimmy helping Kate with the dishes. Pat was sitting in a chair by the old radio. "Could you do me a favour, please, Edward?"

"Sure, Pat."

"You know, I often forget to do things." She smiled. Her eyes were very clear. "Will you tell Fraser I've left him something in a box under the radio?"

"I will, Pat. I'll tell him."

Blue Lightning's horn blasted twice.

"I'll tell him when we get back to look under the radio. Bye, Pat."

I jumped down the steps and ran to the alley. Behind me, the screen door slammed.

CHAPTER 17

STEEL TRUE – BLADE STRAIGHT

Old Fort Point
at the foot of
Tekarra Mountain

Fraser looked up as we bumped onto the bridge below Old Fort Point. "Four hundred feet of rocky promontory," he said, "with sheer cliffs on either side."

"Like giant steps," said Jenny. She dangled her hand in front of her face, making her fingers walk up the meadowed plateaus. "Left, right, left, right – and then you can jump right into the sky."

Blue Lightning crossed the bridge and pulled into the little parking area. Jean reached under the canvas camper and took out the kite and fishing rod, then we scrambled up the cliff until we were on a ridge that looked straight to the top. Behind us, we heard the whistle of a train. Across the valley, to the north, Jasper was nestled against the hill. Above it stood Pyramid Mountain.

We started up the dusty trail. On our left, three miles across, a range of mountains rose from wooded slopes.

"Still sleeping away the ages," said Jean, "Old Man Mountain under his blanket of trees."

"Old Man is part of the Collin Range," said Fraser, "and the Collin Range is part of the Rocky Mountain system. You can't imagine how many ranges there are. They wander into each other from Alaska to Mexico. They're the stony backbone of North America."

"There are millions of trees," I said

"And they're all a long way down, Wiggins. Be careful."

I stared over the cliff, looking down at the tops of the pointed pine trees.

"Is your ankle all right, Jean?" asked Fraser.

"It's fine. Hasn't bothered me for months."

Now the trail cut across to the other side of the first plateau. Straight below us to the west, the river was green and clear as it wound its way north, like a chain of looped silver on the forest floor.

"The Athabasca River is a line of history, Wiggins," said Fraser. "Over there, the original pathfinders built their teepees and pine-bow huts. The spot we're standing on would have been a great place for the fur traders to watch for approaching canoes. And over there, below the Palisades," he pointed to a long wall of mountain that swept away to the east, "that marks the line of the railroad, and now the new highway."

As we hiked up through the sunshine, we came upon a band of big horn sheep. "And remember," Fraser said, "look out for all other living things." The sheep all glanced up calmly as we headed for the top.

We sat on the rocky knoll at the top of Old Fort Point. There were

mountains everywhere, parted by long valleys that led to hidden places. Far below, I could see the iron bridge that spanned the river, and beyond it the winding road that led back to Jasper.

Jean stood up. She shook her head, and her hair bounced around her shoulders. With both arms she hugged herself. Then she lifted her chin and took a deep, deep breath. "Fill me up!" she shouted. She smiled and turned slowly to face us. Then, she started singing.

"I wanna be loved by you."

Jenny and I looked at each other, our mouths wide open.

"Just you and nobody else but you!"

With her hands on her hips, Jean lifted a foot into the air, and used it to push Fraser's shoulder. He fell back on the rock, laughing.

"I wanna be loved by you, alone! Pooh pooh bee doo!"

Now she was staring straight at me.

"I wanna be kissed by you!" She grabbed my T-shirt and pulled me, real close. *"Just you and nobody else but you."* Then she patted Jenny's head and touched the end of her nose with one finger.

"I wanna be kissed by you, alone. Pooh pooh bee doo! I couldn't aspire," Jean was dancing all over the rock, *"to anything higher! Than to fill the desire!"* She threw her arms out, as though to embrace the valley. *"To make you my own! Everybody now!"*

We all started clapping and singing. *"I wanna be loved by you!"*

"Just you! and nobody else but you!" Then we followed Jean, marching down to the first plateau. *"I wanna be loved by you alone!"* And across the valley a million trees were singing.

"OK! Wiggins! Hold the kite high, and when I yell *go*, start running towards the cliff. And when I say *now*, throw 'er up in the air, and I'll head the other way. Are you ready?"

I nodded, holding the kite above my head.

"Go!"

I started running with all my might across the plateau; my throat burned with each breath. When Fraser yelled *now*, I threw the kite up, and it soared like an eagle into the sky, across the valley, until it was a tiny dot fluttering and pulling on the fishing line. The silver reel whirred, and the kite climbed higher and higher.

"Look, Jenny! Look!" cried Jean. "Look at our beautiful kite!"

But Jenny was gone.

Jean screamed. "Jenny!" And the world stopped. "Fraser! Oh, God!" Jean stood at the edge of the cliff. "Jenny! …she's fallen!"

Fraser dropped the fishing rod and the kite dragged it, bouncing over the cliff. It danced 400 feet above the valley floor, and I could not take my eyes from it as it dropped in long awkward jerks.

Now, like Superman, Fraser jumped over the edge, and I peered down. Jenny was lying on a ledge fifteen feet below. There was blood on her face.

Fraser tried to stand, but he staggered.

Jean screamed again. "Fraser! A bear! There's a bear! Behind you!"

Around the corner of the stone shelf came the huge shoulders of a

lumbering animal. My body stiffened. The bear had small eyes and a flat face. Its fur was yellowish brown, with black on its spine and legs. I yelled. "Jenny! Fraser!" I started to cry. The massive humped-back grizzly lurched forward, dragging its claws on the rocky pathway.

Fraser now stood unsteadily between Jenny and the bear. He turned to look beyond where Jenny was just managing to stand. There huddled against the wall of the cliff were two small bear cubs. Jenny and Fraser were between the bawling cubs and their mother. The mother grizzly snorted loudly and raised herself on hind legs. Her fur shook. Suddenly, Fraser fell again clutching his chest. The big bear dropped, then came closer. Fraser was motionless. Jenny grabbed Fraser's collar, trying to drag him. "Go!" she shouted to the bear cubs. "Go!" Now Jenny stood above Fraser and cupped her hands – she was holding out her courage. Again she shouted. "Go! Go!" The bear cubs scrambled over Fraser towards their mother. Still Jenny held her courage. Again the mother bear reared. She snorted and whined, almost as if she were human, dabbing her forepaws into the air. Then she came down and turned towards her cubs. With a final look back, the bears shuffled slowly around the corner and out of sight.

"Edward, we need help!" cried Jean. "We've got to get help!"

I looked down to the valley far below. Moving across the bridge was the black and white gum machine.

I started jumping up and down. "Sergeant Gumbrell! Sergeant Gumbrell!" But the car kept moving.

I tore my T-shirt off and waved it high in the air. "Sergeant Gumbrell!" I shouted. But the gum machine was near the end of the bridge, ready to start up the winding road. In panic, I took a deep breath and opened my mouth wide. I gave my Tarzan yell, and the sound filled my head and spilled from my ears. I kept yelling until I could yell no more. The gum machine stopped. And now Sergeant Gumbrell was bounding up the hill.

"It's all right!" I shouted. "Sergeant Gumbrell is coming. Sergeant Gumbrell is coming!"

Jean cried out, "Stay still, Jenny! Don't move!"

Fraser tried to stand, but fell again to his knees.

"Hurry! Sergeant Gumbrell! Hurry!"

At last he was with us. Gasping for breath, Sergeant Gumbrell shouted, "McKillop! Jenny! Hold on!" He threw off his tunic with the gold buttons, and lowered himself over the cliff. As if she were a feather, he held Jenny high above his head, and Jean and I scrambled to haul her up. There was blood on her face and T-shirt. Then with a mighty heave, Sergeant Gumbrell hoisted Fraser onto his shoulder, like a fireman would, and climbed back up onto the plateau. He placed Fraser gently on the ground.

"Are you OK, Fraser?" Jenny asked. "Are you OK?"

His face was grey, but his lips were moving.

"What's that you say, McKillop?" Sergeant Gumbrell crouched, turning an ear to Fraser's lips.

"Froth," muttered Fraser, "froth and bubbles."

"It's all right, McKillop. Hang on." Sergeant Gumbrell now looked at Jean, as if for the first time. "My goodness – " He seemed surprised. "We meet again."

"I wore a wig at church. You didn't recognize me…." She looked down at Fraser. "We must get him to a doctor – quickly."

"We shall," said Sergeant Gumbrell. "We shall." He picked Fraser up in his arms. "It seems we are destined to visit Seton Hospital again."

"Again I thank you," said Jean. She tried to smile. "But, we must hurry."

Fraser's eyes were still closed, and Jenny held his hand as we started down the hill. Above us, Smoky the crow followed in large descending circles.

"Have courage, Fraser," whispered Jenny. "Have courage."

Seton Hospital smelled of ether and waxed linoleum. It was a still and echoey place. Silent nuns glided in and out of doors as Jean and Sergeant Gumbrell, and Jenny and I sat in the waiting area, staring down a long dark hallway. At the far end a light was shining on a statue of Jesus.

"This is where I had my tonsils out," whispered Jenny. She now had a white bandage on her forehead. "When you get your tonsils out, they give you ice cream."

Sergeant Gumbrell stood. "I'll leave you now," he said, bowing to Jean. "The children's parents should be told."

"Thanks, again, Magnus." She tried to smile. "One year, exactly."

"Glad to be of help. He's not a bad fellow, really." Sergeant Gumbrell turned like a soldier and marched off, his footsteps solid on the shiny floor.

"Did you know Sergeant Gumbrell before?" asked Jenny.

"When I was in Jasper last summer I sprained my ankle. Sergeant Gumbrell drove me to the hospital."

"He's a very nice man."

"He is. But since then, Fraser and he have not gotten along. I think Fraser was jealous."

"I guess Fraser wanted to be your hero."

"He always has been." Jean looked down. Her mouth opened like she was going to cry, but no sound came out.

Down the hallway two figures appeared. Their reflections moved towards us along the linoleum.

"Dr. Venner and Dr. Betkowski."

"We have sad news," said Dr. Betkowski.

Jean gasped. "Fraser?"

"Fraser McKillop will be fine. We'll keep him overnight to be sure. But I'm sorry to tell you that Pat Blossom passed away a few moments ago."

Now another figure stood in front of the bright statue of Jesus. Kate Blossom seemed frail and tiny, leaning heavy on her cane. "My sister," she sobbed. "My dear sister."

Jenny started to cry. I didn't know what to do.

CHAPTER 18

SLOW MOTION DANCE

For three days, no one came or went from the Donald Duck House. There was no smoke from Fraser's garage. Only Smoky the crow continued his daily habit of gathering stale bread and throwing it into the fountain.

With her notebook open, Jenny sat cross-legged on Mountaintop Rock.

"What are you writing?" I asked.

"Nothing. I've never known anyone who died. Have you?"

"My Uncle Frank was very sick once."

Jenny and I sat quietly, looking up and down the alley.

As the siren at the fire hall blew, the gum machine pulled up to the Dinky toy sandpit. Blue Lightning was right behind it. Fraser, Jean, and Kate stepped from the truck as Sergeant Gumbrell got out of the police car. Fraser and Sergeant Gumbrell were now talking.

"The show must go on," said Fraser. He and Sergeant Gumbrell shook hands, while Kate smiled sadly. In her free arm, she held a grey stone jar.

Jean was smiling up at us. "It's a sad day, but the sun is still shining."

Jenny looked down to the empty page of her notebook.

"Jenny never knew anyone who died," I said, lifting my hand to her knee.

Jean placed her hand on Jenny's other knee. "Was anything so common, so awesome. It happens everyday. It happens." She stopped. "Aunt Pat has been cremated, and we hope you and your parents will join us for a short ceremony."

Jenny looked up. "Cremated. What does that mean?"

Jean considered her reply. "When a person dies – and all the lovely things they are have flown to heaven – when their body is an empty shell, then it's turned to ashes."

"Ashes?"

Jean nodded. "When the spirit has left the body, then the body is burned." She reached up and hugged us. I felt her warm and soft against me.

"Tomorrow, we're putting Aunt Pat's ashes into Lac Beauvert."

I stared into Jean's eyes. Then she turned and walked away.

"There must be lots of lovely things in heaven," said Jenny, wiping her cheek. "It must be a beautiful place." She picked up her pencil and began writing again.

We met at the small bay beside the 14th golf tee on Lac Beauvert. The water was as still as glass, and all around, the pine trees reached out to touch each other. There was a clean smell of morning in the air.

"Thank you for coming," said Fraser. He was wearing his tweed jacket and tartan tie. He shook hands with Mrs. Trotwood, and my mom and dad, and then told Jenny and me he appreciated our being

there. Jean held Kate's arm, as Kate cradled the stone jar. She gazed across the lake. On the other side, the stone giant looked down from a blue sky.

"My eulogy is short," Fraser said. He gently took the jar from Kate's arm. "Patricia Blossom loved Jasper. She was a true pioneer. She was loved by all." He took the top from the jar and Kate lifted out some ashes.

"As in the eye of nature she has lived," said Kate, "so in the eye of nature, let her die." She threw the ashes onto the lake, and they drifted down, wobbling from side-to-side, through the glinting water.

Now we all held hands, and there was only the sound of a bee buzzing in a wild rose bush.

Jenny squeezed my hand. "Look," she whispered.

I squinted into the water. From the dark depths, a long grey shape appeared. It moved towards us like a slow torpedo.

Jenny squeezed harder. "It's the big rainbow."

The huge trout turned right in front of us. Its body flashed with captured sunshine. It glinted green and blue and pink as it moved through the ashes, its mouth gaping like a hole in an old sock. As it swam, the water stirred, and the ashes lifted and rolled in a dreamy slow motion dance. Then with no apparent thrust of fins or body, the fish turned again and disappeared into the deep water.

As we drove home, large clouds billowed in the west, and it started to rain.

CHAPTER 19

LA FEMME FAMEUSE

It was still raining the next morning when Jenny and I met at Mountaintop Rock. We stood, splashing our gumboots into mud puddles and listening to the rain make music on our plastic raincoats. It was the last Saturday of the summer. We planned on going to the show and then to the school gymnasium to see *South Pacific*.

"My mom says I can take my bandage off before school starts," said Jenny. She touched her forehead.

"Are you nervous about school?" I asked.

"No. Are you?"

"A little."

"We'll learn lots of interesting things."

"Will they teach us about Henry House?"

"We don't learn about Jasper in school."

We splashed up the alley to the Blossom sisters'. Through the gate in the hedge, we saw Jean going into Fraser's garage. She was carrying her two small suitcases.

I followed Jenny along the wet path to the Oak Book Barrel. It was now covered with canvas. Straining our ears, we tried to catch a picture of what was happening inside. The fire in the stove was crackling.

"I've said goodbye to Aunt Kate," we heard Jean say. "She's gone to the gym to finish painting the set. They've all gone, Joan and Honoria, Reg and Tom. Aren't you going?"

"Not in the mood," said Fraser.

"You always did whatever you wanted."

"So did you."

There was a pause, and the fire sputtered. "You don't have to leave," said Fraser. "We could make it work."

"Maybe if you lived in LA, Fraser, or my life was here in the mountains. But it's not." Jean sounded like a little girl again. "Our timing – it's all wrong."

Jenny and I crouched by the barrel as Fraser appeared at the door with the suitcases. Now they were walking towards the gate. As they stepped into the alley, Jimmy Herron's big car pulled up.

"The timing is perfect," said Fraser, "for whatever is meant to be."

Jean kissed his wet cheek. "I just wanted to be someone else for a while."

Suddenly Jenny shouted out, "You don't have to go, Jean! You can stay."

Jean stared through the drizzle. "Oh, Jenny. I do love Jasper. But the things I want, I can't find here." She bent down and kissed each of us on the cheek. "You guys will always be my two best sweethearts in the whole world."

"Will we see you again?" I asked.

"Keep smiling, Edward, and I'll always be with you." She looked sad as she got into the car.

As Fraser closed the door, a train whistle blew in the west yard. Two long, then a short, then a long.

"Goodbye, Jean," said Fraser. He lifted his shoulders against the rain. "I'll be watching for you, up there in the stars."

As the big car drove away, Jean's hand was small and white at the window.

Fraser still stared down the alley after the car had disappeared. Then he looked at Jenny and me like he had just noticed we were there. He gave us a tired smile. "How's that bump on your head, Jenny?"

"My mom says the bandages will be off before school starts."

"Ah, that's great. Then you're on the mend. Thanks again for everything." He walked back along the wet path.

Jenny and I stood at the Blossom sisters' gate in the rain. The pond was now overflowing, and the fountain had no purpose as it splashed high into the air.

"Fraser, wait!" Jenny reached into her pocket. She ran and handed him the letter from Sir Arthur Conan Doyle. He looked at the folded letter curiously, then smiled like he recognized it as one of Jenny's lists. He put the letter into his shirt pocket, then placed one hand over top, protecting it.

"Thanks, Jenny." Fraser wiped splattered raindrops from his face and went into his garage.

We never went to the show that afternoon. Standing in front of the Chaba Theatre, we quickly examined the photographs that showed highlights of the movie.

"Starring Cary Grant," said Jenny, staring up at the marquee. "I've never heard of him."

Grey rain had turned to pale sunshine, and now across Connaught Drive we saw a huge crowd on the station platform. Hundreds of people were gathered around the Trans Continental. Above the crowd, we saw a flash of gold. In the vestibule of the first coach stood a small figure. It was Jean.

Jenny and I ran to the totem pole and watched as the crowd grew bigger. "Jean!" shouted Jenny. "Jean!"

Jean looked up and waved. People were trying to touch her and hold her hand. They grabbed her clothes and pulled on her. Suddenly she slipped and started to fall into the crowd. Jimmy Herron was behind her and pulled her back.

Now Jean stared out over all the heads that were staring up at her. She tried to smile, but couldn't. With a fragile look, she bowed her head and cupped her hands; Jenny did the same. Then Jean disappeared into the coach.

"She's gone," I said.

Jenny was staring up at all the mythical animals. "What shall we do now?"

As if by magic, the crowd started to disappear. People moved off in all directions. Now there was no one around the vestibule of the first coach.

Jenny slapped my shoulder. "Gotcha last!" She ran around the totem pole. I chased her. We kept running, round and round, until Jenny suddenly stopped. Sitting on the low stone wall that bordered the platform was a lady. She was wearing blue jeans, a sweatshirt, and running shoes. On her lap were some sandwiches wrapped in wax paper. She looked to the platform, then to us, then back to the platform.

"You're from Québec," said Jenny. "You're going to be a school teacher."

"I am," said the lady. She offered us a sandwich.

"Are you looking for Sergeant Gumbrell?"

"The sergeant, he said he would meet me."

"He's been looking for you every day."

"But not today?"

"He's at the school gymnasium. We could take you."

"But the train is about to leave."

"Why don't you just stay?"

"My classes, they start next week." She looked above our heads and then reached out as if she was trying to touch something far away. She smiled. "If I could grasp la roche sentinelle, I would take it home with me."

I looked back at Pyramid Mountain standing guard above the town.

"You are lucky to live here in the mountains," said the lady from Québec. She folded the wax paper, then took a white handkerchief from her pocket and wiped her hands.

"Do you *have* to go?" asked Jenny.

"I do."

"So did Jean."

"Jean?"

Jenny looked to the windows of the first coach. "She's going to New York."

"Ah, la femme fameuse."

"All aboard!" shouted the conductor.

The lady from Québec walked quickly to the vestibule of the first coach.

"Maybe we'll meet again," I shouted.

The big wheels turned, and the steam whistle blew. The Trans Continental reared high above the platform.

"To the future!" said the lady from Québec. "A l'avenir. Voila une journée memorable!"

As the train pulled away, a small white hand waved from a dark window.

Sergeant Gumbrell was singing at the top of his lungs as Jenny and I entered the crowded gymnasium. He was center stage, dressed in white trousers, a white shirt, and a flat hat wrapped with blue ribbon. He was standing on a desert island, although above him, suspended from the stage, was a basketball hoop. Somewhere in the wings, the Frank Darlow Orchestra was playing.

"It's loud!" Jenny yelled in my ear.

Mrs. Trotwood now appeared, wearing a billowy dress decorated with flowers. As she started to sing, a long line of sailors danced out behind her. At the same time, the paper mâché volcano rolled onto the stage.

> *"I'm as corny as Kansas in August,*
> *High as a flag on the Fourth of July!*
> *If you'll excuse an expression I use,*
> *I'm in love, I'm in love, I'm in love,*
> *I'm in love, I'm in love with a wonderful guy!"*

Cymbals crashed and trumpets blared. The net on the basketball

hoop shook uncontrollably. Smoke puffed from the volcano, and the gymnasium filled with thunderous applause. In the front row we saw Kate and Mr. Trotwood, and my mom and dad clapping and cheering. As the sailors on stage raised their hats, Mrs. Trotwood and Sergeant Gumbrell smiled graciously and took their bows.

"It's finished," said Jenny. "The volcano is finished. Shall we go, now?"

CHAPTER 20

THE MESSAGE IN THE BOX

The eerie yellow light twisted above the trap door and the man with the grey moustache glared down from the photo as Jenny and I crept into Fraser's garage. As we stepped down into the room with gold wallpaper, violin music came up to meet us. The music stopped, and we heard a voice.

"To Sherlock Holmes she was always *the* woman."

"Dr. Watson," Jenny whispered.

The voice continued. "When Holmes refers to her photograph, he seldom mentions her by any other name."

Jenny put her lips close to my ear. "*The* woman was Sherlock's true love, the only person ever to outwit him."

Again the violin played. It was spooky, but kind of sad.

Jenny raised her hand to knock on the middle door. "Should I?"

"I guess."

The music stopped with a gentle squawk. "Never guess, Wiggins! It's a shocking habit, destructive to the logical faculty."

Jenny pushed the door open.

"The Great Detective said that in the 'The Sign of Four.' A wonderful story. You should read it." Fraser was standing in front of the fire wearing the purple dressing gown. In his left hand he held a violin; in his right, the bow for stroking it. On the mantel in front of the mirror

was a photograph of Jean. She was standing on a ledge above Athabasca Falls, tons of white water crashing all around her. Above the ledge, in the trees, was Blue Lightning.

"Close the door," said Fraser. "You'll let the dust in. And welcome to the sitting room of Sherlock Holmes."

"We've been here before," said Jenny.

"I know," Fraser said, glancing at the photograph.

There was silence, as if no one knew what to say.

"Are you sad Jean left?" asked Jenny.

"I could be, if I wanted to." He put the violin on the table with all the test tubes and the bottles.

"I think I know where you go every night. I think I've guessed that mystery."

"Not every night," said Fraser, "but most nights, Blue Lightning and I make our little trip."

"We won't tell anybody, will we?" said Jenny, looking at me. I agreed to what ever it was we weren't going to tell.

"I'm sure your dad would frown," Fraser said, "if he knew someone was digging tunnels under the alley. And he'd be particularly upset about dumping the dirt over Athabasca Falls." He struck a match and started a small flame under a beaker of clear liquid. "Have a seat, and we'll have a cup of tea."

While the flame heated the water in the beaker, Fraser went to the mantel and picked up the letter from Sir Arthur Conan Doyle. "Where did you get this, Jenny?"

"We found it at the end of the tunnel. It was in a paint box."

"A paint box?"

"It was sticking out of the dirt."

"A box!" I said, jumping up. "Pat said there was another box."

"Another box?" said Fraser. "What box? How many boxes?"

I tried to explain. "The letter from Sir Arthur Conan Doyle was in a paint box, but Pat said she left you a box under the radio in the porch. I forgot to tell you."

We followed Fraser quickly into the room with gold wallpaper. Instead of taking the steps to the garage, he opened the third door. It entered into a passage at the other end of which, narrow steps went up to the ceiling. Fraser climbed the steps and thumped his fist hard on a trap door. The door popped open, and Fraser's head and shoulders disappeared into the Blossom sisters' back porch. When he came down, he was holding a small metal box.

"A battered tin box," he said, "like the one Dr. Watson used to hold the adventures of Sherlock Holmes."

Back in the sitting room we sat on the couch as Fraser poured cups of tea. The bright flames on the fire splashed orange and gold light onto the tin box.

"Open it," said Fraser. "Let's see what's inside."

Jenny pushed back the clasp and lifted the lid. Staring up at us was a man with a big grey moustache, a photograph.

"Sir Arthur Conan Doyle," I said. "Like the picture upstairs in the garage."

"No, Wiggins." Fraser picked up the photo. "This isn't Sir Arthur. The man upstairs is Sir Arthur. This man is my grandfather."

"Daisy!" exclaimed Jenny. "Constable Alfred Daisy Blossom of the Northwest Mounted Police. Sir Arthur's letter was to him, but why wasn't it mailed?"

Fraser gazed at the photograph. "The news of my grandfather's death came on June 22nd, 1914. It came from England by wire, just as my mother, Kate and Pat were seeing the Doyles off at the train station. The telegram read, *Alfred Blossom, Special Agent, died in the arms of his loving wife, on the steps of the village church in Hindhead, Surrey.* My grandfather died from a heart attack."

"He was a Special Agent?"

Fraser nodded.

Jenny was staring into the fire. "Do you think he found the great creator?"

"My grandfather was booked to sail to Europe the next day. He was being sent by the British Foreign Office to Belgium. Daisy Blossom was a remarkable mediator. He might have made a difference."

"A difference to what?"

Fraser paused, as if thinking about the question. Then he said softly, "June 28th, 1914. Fifty years of aggressive nationalism went into making Europe an inflammatory place. A few days were enough to detonate it."

"June 28th, 1914. Is that an important date?"

Fraser looked deep into Jenny's eyes. "It doesn't matter right now, on a quiet leafy day like this. Summer's almost over. There's lots of time to learn about things like that."

He reached into the box again and took out some pieces of folded writing paper.

"Is it the rest of the story?" asked Jenny.

Fraser shook his head. He read.

"*To my nephew Fraser,*

I write quickly. This wretched disease robs me of my mind.

They say it is not right to rake up the past. But how can we get at it unless we dig a little. The present has such a rough way of treading it down.

I am lost. I cannot take a thought and complete it. The box before you belonged to your mother. She said Sir Arthur gave it to her.

Winnie was always the favourite.

I never forgave your mother for stealing your father from me. Always the baby. Special baby. But then there would not have been you.

Winnie said Sir Arthur gave her the story. She would not let us read it. Why should he give it to her?

We made our kite in Colonel Rogers' living room, at the Boulders. Sir Arthur let us use his discarded pages. When no one was looking I took some pages from Winnie's story and glued them onto the frame of the kite. When we flew the kite from Old Fort Point, I let it go. I let it go. Winnie was Daddy's favourite. Always the special baby.

But, I read the story, and I know where Henry House is. I will tell you."

"Fraser!" said Jenny.

"Not now, Jenny! Hold on till the end.

"*You must first go to Old Fort Point.*"

"But, Fraser!"

"Not now, Jenny! This *is* the location of Henry House."

Jenny grabbed the letter from his hand. "Look!" she said, pointing up.

"What?"

From a long jagged crack in the ceiling, a steady stream of sand was pouring onto the floor.

"Get out of here!" shouted Fraser. He shoved us towards the door.

In the room with gold wallpaper, Fraser threw back the grey canvas. As he did, our ears were filled with a deafening crash. It thundered at us from down the tunnel, pushing a giant cloud of billowing dust into our faces.

"It's caving in!" cried Fraser. Jenny screamed. The lights went out. "I've got you, Jenny. It's all right."

I turned frantically in the darkness searching for the steps, but collided with Fraser and Jenny. I was drowning in dust.

"The porch, Wiggins. Get to the porch!"

Coughing, I groped for the handle of the third door. Furniture was smashing and glass breaking in the sitting room. I pushed on the third door and felt dust shoot ahead of me into the passage.

"Go!" yelled Fraser. "Go!"

We ran down the passage, rocks falling behind us. I flew up the steps and hit the trap door with my shoulder. I hit it again and again, but it didn't budge. Suddenly, Fraser's hand thumped hard beside me. The door popped, and we scrambled to the safety of the Blossom sister's porch.

Sucking air into our lungs, we stared through the mosquito screen into the bright sunshine. Everything in the yard was normal except for a thin cloud of dust drifting from the open door of Fraser's garage.

"The alley," gasped Jenny, "what about the alley?"

The alley was normal except for Mountaintop Rock. What had been a boulder was now a low flat stone on the edge of the vacant lot.

"It didn't cave," Fraser said. "The alley didn't cave."

"We won't tell anyone, will we?" said Jenny. As she said that, the letter that Pat had written fell from her pocket. She bent to pick it up, but a loud squawk stopped her. Swooping down, Smoky snatched the letter with his beak. With a clap and a whistle of wings, he flew up and over the Blossom sisters' hedge.

"No!" yelled Fraser. "Smoky! No!"

We ran to the gate. In the fountain, Smoky was hopping up and down and flapping his wings. He threw the letter high into the air; the water was splashing all around him.

"Hell's bells!" shouted Fraser. He ran to the fountain, and Smoky shot off like an arrow. Fraser plunged his arm into the water and grabbed the letter, but as he lifted it out it slipped through his fingers like wet slithery porridge. "No!" he cried. "No!" The location of Henry House had dissolved in the Blossom sisters' pond.

"It's goop," said Jenny. "Just goop."

"What's goop?" asked a voice from the alley.

Mr. Trotwood was at the gate. Behind him stood Mrs. Trotwood,

who was still wearing her billowy dress decorated with flowers, and Sergeant Gumbrell, still in his stage makeup and sailor costume. Now the grey Chevy pulled up to the Dinky toy sandpit. Kate and my mom and dad got out.

"It was a letter from Pat," explained Jenny. "She wrote it to Fraser, but he couldn't read it because Smoky threw it into the pond. And we found a story about Sherlock Holmes, by Sir Arthur Conan Doyle. He typed it on Colonel Rogers' typewriter."

"What?" said Mr. Trotwood.

"Sherlock discovered where William Henry built the original Henry House. But Pat glued the story to a kite and flew it from the top of Old Fort Point."

"But, Jenny."

"She let the kite go. But she read the story first, and she knew the location."

"Jenny."

"She *knew* the location of Henry House."

"Jenny, Sir Arthur Conan Doyle never used a typewriter."

"What?"

"Sir Arthur Conan Doyle never once in his life used a typewriter to write his stories. I read it in a magazine. Doyle wrote everything long hand."

"Aye, that's a fact," said Dad. "The Great Detective's knowledge of typewriters helped him to solve cases, but his creator never used one."

"But then, who wrote 'The Mystery of Henry House?'"

There was a loud caw from the roof of the garage as Smoky the crow rose on his broad black wings. He circled the vacant lot once and then flew swiftly out across the railroad tracks toward Tekarra Mountain.

"I don't know, Jenny," said Mr. Trotwood. "I'm sure, I don't know." Then Mr. Trotwood saw the flat stone that had once been Mountaintop Rock. "The boulder – " We all stared.

"A sinkhole?" said Dad. "Caused by the rain? Can ye imagine?"

"But the whole boulder?" Mr. Trotwood lifted his hat and scratched his head.

"Nature always seems to find what it's looking for," said Kate. She smiled at no one in particular. "Human beings aren't always so lucky." Her eyes settled on Fraser. "I think we should all have a nice cup of tea. Don't you?"

"A cup of tea!" said Mrs. Trotwood. She gave Jenny a big hug. "Yes! And we'll tell you all about our great performance."

"Wonderful!" shouted Sergeant Gumbrell. "As wonderful as the evening I sang with the great Bing Crosby."

Fraser was still staring down the alley. "A nice cup of tea." He smiled, giving Jenny a quick wink. "Let's all have a nice cup of tea."

Everyone followed Kate into the yard as I watched Smoky the crow climb higher and higher into the sky. Soon he was just a tiny pinprick in a big white cloud. Then, when he was right above Old Fort Point, I blinked and he disappeared.

ORDER ON MOUNTAINTOP ROCK FROM THE OAK BARREL BOOK SHOP.

Please send _____ copies of *On Mountaintop Rock* to:

Name _____

Street _____

City _____

Province/State _____ Postal/Zip Code _____

Enclosed is $19.95 per book plus $5.00 for shipping and GST. (Total $24.95)

Total amount enclosed is _____

Make cheque or money order payable to **Cobblestone Creek**
6528 – 112 Street
Edmonton, Alberta
Canada   T6H 4R2

· ·

ORDER ON MOUNTAINTOP ROCK FROM THE OAK BARREL BOOK SHOP.

Please send _____ copies of *On Mountaintop Rock* to:

Name _____

Street _____

City _____

Province/State _____ Postal/Zip Code _____

Enclosed is $19.95 per book plus $5.00 for shipping and GST. (Total $24.95)

Total amount enclosed is _____

Make cheque or money order payable to **Cobblestone Creek**
6528 – 112 Street
Edmonton, Alberta
Canada   T6H 4R2

· ·

ORDER ON MOUNTAINTOP ROCK FROM THE OAK BARREL BOOK SHOP.

Please send _____ copies of *On Mountaintop Rock* to:

Name _____

Street _____

City _____

Province/State _____ Postal/Zip Code _____

Enclosed is $19.95 per book plus $5.00 for shipping and GST. (Total $24.95)

Total amount enclosed is _____

Make cheque or money order payable to **Cobblestone Creek**
6528 – 112 Street
Edmonton, Alberta
Canada   T6H 4R2

Again Jean breathed in the cool night air. "Look at all the stars, Fraser. Millions and millions of stars."

To order a copy of *On Mountaintop Rock* for a friend: send a cheque or money order for $19.95 plus, $5.00 for shipping and GST. (Total: $24.95)

To all their friends,
Jenny and Edward say *hello*.

And please remember to keep bears wild and don't feed them garbage

Order forms are back of this page.